THE CHAINS OF DESIRE

BOOKS BY CLARK

THE STAINS OF TIME

OTHER BOOKS

THE CHAINS OF DESIRE

E. CHRISTOPHER CLARK

Published in the United States by Clarkwoods in Chelmsford, Massachusetts.

This is a work of fiction. Names, characters, places, and incidents either are the product of the author's imagination or are used fictitiously, and any resemblance to any actual persons, living or dead, events, or locales is entirely coincidental.

ISBN for the Print Edition: 978-1-952044-22-9
ISBN for the Digital Edition: 978-1-952044-23-6

Library of Congress Control Number: 2020917645

For Dexter, Travis, Berklee, and every other girl I've ever crushed on

❧ I ❧
EVERYTHING'S WAITING
FOR YOU

1990-1995

Sixteen years before she was killed, in the aftermath of her parents' first divorce, Robin Gates found a copy of her obituary.

She was twelve, it was February vacation, and her mother had picked up a shift at the bar to make rent. Robin was supposed to be keeping an eye on her little brother, but Adam was glued to the Ms. Pac-Man machine in the corner—and had been ever since the barkeep handed him a mug full of quarters. If Adam was occupied, Robin was supposed to be up on the stage with her guitar—and a mug of her own to collect tips. But she hated the way the dirty old men leered at her while she played, as if the guitar and the stage made even a sixth grader fair game, so she grabbed a newspaper and sat in a booth near the fireplace. Robin sat and waited.

"Why don't you do your part?" her mother would ask her. "Why don't you do your part to keep a roof over our heads?"

"We *have* a roof over our heads," she planned to say, "when we're at Dad's." And the biting snark of the retort she'd lined up was enough to make Robin smile.

Until, that is, she caught sight of her name on the front page of the paper—*her* name, Robin Gates—under the headline "Local Singer Shot Dead."

> *Robin Gates, the Chelmsford native whose song "Precious Whore" and its accompanying music video skyrocketed her to international fame in the late 90s—*

Late 90s? thought Robin. *It's only 1990 right now.*

She was about to check the dateline on the article when the whole paper was torn from her hands. "Hey!" she shouted, but her mother had crumpled the whole thing into a ball before Robin could say "give it back."

"If you have time to read," said her mother, "then you have time to play."

Robin leapt to her feet, then leapt to grab at the balled-up wad of newsprint her mother held high overhead. "I need to finish reading that."

"Hey," shouted the barkeep, "no horsing around near the fireplace, for Christ's sake."

"Stop it," said Robin's mother, twisting this way and that to keep the prize out of reach.

"You'll split your skull open," shouted the barkeep, making his way toward them. "Or immolate yourself if you ain't careful."

"Stop acting like a child," said Robin's mother, nudge-shoving her daughter back into the booth.

"Hey," said the barkeep, stepping in between them. "Let's keep it civil, alright? You got family problems, you take 'em outside."

"No problem," said Robin's mother, with a curt little bow to the barkeep.

The barkeep ruffled Robin's hair and gave her a smile. "Don't make your ma hire a babysitter, huh? Things are tight enough for you guys as it is."

She nodded. Then she watched, powerless, as her mother threw the paper into the flames. But Robin had a plan. There was a whole stack of other newspapers where she got that one, and there had to be another copy.

There just had to be.

ROBIN PLAYED FOR A HALF-HOUR, collected her tips, and then handed over the wad of bills to her mother. Seemingly placated now, the older woman said nothing when her daughter made a beeline for the piled newspapers stacked near the entrance. And the barkeep, that asshole accomplice, had nothing to say either—not even when Robin gathered every paper there was into her arms. All he had to offer her was a shake of his head and a roll of his tired eyes.

As she passed her brother and his video game on the way back to the table, Adam pleaded with Robin not to get them kicked out. "I'm about to beat the high score," he said. "Don't ruin everything like you usually do."

"Fuck you," she said, speaking the curse aloud for the first time in her life and liking the feel of it on her tongue.

THERE WASN'T another copy of the paper she was looking for, but Robin found papers from all over the world in the pile—and from all across time. Nothing else from the future, though, and that's really what she wanted to see most of all: something to prove she wasn't insane.

"You're not," said a voice from above her.

"Not what?" said Robin, and then she looked up from her reading to see who was speaking to her. It was a waitress—one of her mother's coworkers, Robin presumed, though this one looked like she was dressed for Halloween. She was wearing a ruffled bodice, a corset, and a skirt far longer than the one Mom was wearing.

"You're not crazy," said the waitress. "That's what you were thinking, wasn't it?"

"How do you know what I was thinking?" asked Robin.

The waitress laughed. "I watched you dig through that pile like a woman on a mission. And then," she said, shaking her head as she smiled, "the look on your poor face when you didn't find it..."

"I didn't find it," said Robin, "because it doesn't exist."

"Why do you say that?" said the waitress.

"Because you can't read a paper from the future!" said Robin, at a volume a little closer to a shout than she'd intended. The barkeep, she noticed, had taken a sudden interest in their conversation. He'd drifted over the side of the bar closest to the two of them.

The waitress took a seat opposite Robin and pulled the stack of papers toward her. "But," said the waitress, "what if you can?"

"You can't," said Robin. "I just imagined it."

"But what if you didn't?" asked the waitress. She was thumbing through an issue of the *Boston Globe* from 1918. "What if, in here—in this place—you *can* see the future?"

Robin was about to ask what made this place—this *dive*—special, but then she thought of the headline again. *Local Singer Shot Dead.* And so, instead of asking her question, she just said: "I don't want the future I saw."

"Are you sure?" asked the waitress.

"The newspaper said I was going to die," said Robin.

"We're all going to die," said the waitress with a chuckle, and she rubbed at the back of her neck.

"It said I was going to be shot."

The waitress said nothing for a second, just nodded somberly as she stared down at the table. Then she looked up and faced Robin again. "What else did it say?"

"It said I'm gonna be famous."

The waitress smiled. "That doesn't sound so bad," she said. "Famous for what?"

"For my music," said Robin.

"And do you like playing?"

"Hey," shouted the barkeep, who was rounding the corner of the bar now. "Ada, what'd I tell you about sticking to your section?"

"I'm sorry, sir," said the waitress. "Just thought the kid could use some cheering up."

"You let her mother worry about that," said the barkeep, collecting the newspapers now and tossing the whole lot into the fire. "And you get back to where you belong."

The barkeep stalked off, grabbing the mug of quarters off the Ms. Pac-Man machine as he stepped back behind the bar. Then he shouted: "Last call."

The waitress frowned as she stood. "Sorry, kid," she said. "Wish I could've helped a bit more, but..." She trailed off, nodding over her shoulder at the now-flustered barkeep.

"Well," said Robin, "I think Mom's picking up another shift tomorrow. Maybe I can find you in your section. I didn't even realize this place was that big. Looks so small from the street."

"Bigger on the inside," said the waitress with a wink, but Robin didn't catch the reference.

"So, maybe tomorrow?" she said.

The waitress looked across the room at the barkeep. And now, if Robin wasn't mistaken, it looked like the waitress might be ready to cry.

"Ada?" said Robin, not entirely sure she'd gotten the waitress' name right.

"Maybe," she said. Then she turned to face Robin one last time, and any tears that might have been there were all gone. "But, just in case we don't catch up," she said, "I want you to remember this one thing."

"What?" said Robin.

"You know now what your future is *supposed* to be," said the waitress, "but when have you ever done things the way you were supposed to?"

◌⁙◌

WHEN ROBIN, her brother, and her mother made the hike out to the bar the next afternoon, they were startled to find a padlock on the door and a sign in the window.

"What do they mean by 'closed permanently'?" asked Adam. "Do they mean, like, *forever?*"

Mom was too busy staring through the window and mumbling to herself to answer her son, so Robin told Adam: "Yes, stupid. That's what it means."

"But I was so close," whined Adam. "I'd finally figured it out! I just needed, like, two more quarters."

Robin's mother told her to go check the side, so that's what Robin did next. And though that door was locked too, Robin lingered for a moment when she saw a single garbage can they seemed to have left behind. And she lingered for one moment beyond that when she saw two words scrawled out on the lid in what looked like charcoal: OPEN ME.

Robin lifted the lid from the trash can and couldn't believe what she saw. There, sitting atop a heap of ash, was a sliver of the newspaper she'd read the night before. It wasn't much more than the headline—the rest had been burned away—but she finally saw the date.

September 29, 2006. That was the day she was going to die.

Robin started to cry. How could it be real? Just *how?*

She was shaking her head in disbelief when she saw a second scrap of newsprint that had survived the fire. She fished it out of the refuse, read it once to herself, then read it once more aloud— not even caring now if Adam or Mom overheard her.

Gates died just outside her apartment building in Cambridge, Massachusetts. She spent her final moments in the arms of Hannah Hamilton, the on-again off-again girlfriend who Gates called "the love of her life" and whose photo graced the cover of the singer's final album "A Hand That Will Never Be a Fist."

"The love of my life," Robin said to herself. And then she said it again. And, as absurd as it was, just the idea of love made her sniffle back the last of her tears and wipe her eyes with her sleeve.

She was going to die, yes. But first she was going to fall in love.

 ❦ 2 ❦

On Easter Sunday that year, in a house clear across town, Ashley Silver stole the new video game from her brother's basket. Then she pointed to the baseball player on the front of the package and proclaimed to her family that she wanted to be a designated hitter.

Mum was already back to sleep in her arm chair. Michael, Ashley's brother, just rolled his eyes. But Dad, at least, had something to say.

As they sat on the living room floor and reached for the Nintendo's controllers, he told her the sad truth: there was no DH in Little League.

"Well, poop," said Ashley. "I just want to hit things."

Behind her, she heard a grunt. Then, under his breath, her brother mumbled "You like to throw stuff at people, too."

"So what," she said, hurling the game's instructions at his head.

"So," said Michael, catching the booklet before it hit him square in the face, "be a pitcher. In Little League, the pitcher bats. Just like in the NL."

"That's right," said their father, sounding surprised that his son knew anything about the game. Then, quickly, he turned to Ashley. "But," he told his daughter, "the goal is *not* to hit the batter. You know that, right?"

She smiled at him, a devilish grin. Then she asked if she could at least make the batter *think* she was going to hit them. And when Dad didn't respond, Ashley shook her eyebrows up and down at him. She made her eyebrows dance like a pair of twin imps upon her forehead, like she was Kevin McAllister in *Home Alone* and she'd just realized she had the power to make her family disappear.

Ashley's father shook his head at her, then mussed her hair.

AND THIS, as it happened, was how Ashley Silver met Robin Gates.

Because their fathers had gone to high school together, Ashley ended up on the team that Mr. Gates coached. No one else was willing to take on a kid who was 10 already, almost 11, and who had never swung a bat—any kid, let alone a *girl*. But Mr. Gates was special. That's what Ashley's dad told her.

He was a great guy, that Phil. "Sold me my first dime bag," said Ashley's father wistfully, forgetting it was his daughter he was talking to, forgetting the 'Just Say No' pamphlets she brought home from school each year. "And look what he's turned himself into," he continued. "Only game in town these days. Keeps the rougher sorts on the other side of the tracks, so to speak. Which gets him in good with the cops, o'course. That and the 'donations' to the force," he said, making quotation marks with his fingers as he said 'donations,' then laughing at his own cleverness—at the innuendo Ashley didn't even understand. And might not have even heard, he realized once he stopped chuckling, given her tendency to tune him out.

Standing by the bleachers on opening day, at the fields on

Route 110 where all the league games were played, the fathers shook hands and introduced their kids to one another.

The kids who were there, that is: Ashley, Robin, and Robin's brother Adam.

"I'd introduce you to my son Michael too," said Ashley's father, "but he's off to the comic book store."

At the words 'comic book,' Adam finally looked up from the ground and joined the conversation. "Which one?" he asked. "Does he go to Hot Comix or the Splash Page?"

"He can't ever decide," said Ashley. "Dad hates us trying to cross the street, but—"

"This road's a mess," said her father, nodding. "Always has been."

"They need a light," said Robin's dad.

"A couple," said Ashley's. "For sure."

"So, if he's crossing the street," said Adam, "that means he goes to the Splash Page."

"He goes back and forth," said Ashley. Then she rolled her eyes. "My brother buys from whichever guy'll give him the better deal. Like a jerk. Even though Eddie and Alice—"

"At the Splash Page," said Adam, interrupting, "you should only ever buy from Alice—"

"Cause she's cute?" said his father, punching Adam in the arm.

"No," said Adam. "Because she'll haggle, even though Eddie won't."

"You know," said his dad, clapping a hand on Adam's shoulder and trying to steer the conversation back to baseball, "Mr. Silver's brother played football for the Lions back in the day. *Legend* in his time. Would've had a big career in college if it weren't for the war."

"That's for sure," said Ashley's dad, though he had no idea. He'd only ever been to one of his brother's games, the last one, and he'd only seen the first quarter. He was ejected from the stadium by his parents after he yelled "Baby killer!" at the players after one of the touchdowns, so angry at his brother for enlisting in the service—not even waiting to see if he'd be drafted, but fucking *enlisting*—that he couldn't stop himself.

"And Mr. Silver's nephew," Robin's father continued, "was Matty Silver."

But the name didn't ring any bells for Adam, who stood there with his mouth open like a codfish.

"The shortstop?" said his dad, shaking Adam's shoulder. "He basically won the team the championship last year?"

"Well, not single-handedly," said Ashley's father, doing what he always did when he sensed tension: trying to deflate it with a laugh.

"What do *you* play?" Robin asked Mr. Silver then, smiling at him. Because when *she* sensed tension, she flirted. Even back then, when she had just barely figured out what flirting was.

"Bass," he said, and he laughed. "Or, well, I used to. Never was all that athletic. Ran track for a couple of seasons, but that's about it."

"Robin's taking up guitar," said her father, setting his hands upon her shoulders now. "Great singer, too. Gonna letter in band once she gets to the high school."

"You can letter in *band*?" Ashley asked, incredulous.

Her father laughed. Then, after a beat, Robin's did too. Yes, you *could* letter in band. And Robin *would*. But that didn't mean the two men couldn't laugh together at the absurdity of it, if only for a moment.

"We better watch out for these girls," Robin's father said to Ashley's. "Your daughter's got a wit on her."

Ashley's father nodded. Then he pointed at Robin and said she was the spitting image of her mother, and everyone knew what a looker she was.

"Little less exotic," said Robin's father. "Got enough of me in her to fit in when she needs to," he said.

If only my brother were that lucky. That's what Robin was thinking.

And what's wrong with exotic? thought Ashley.

❧

LONG BEFORE SHE was on MTV singing about being someone's precious whore, Robin was just this half-Filipino girl that everyone had a crush on. She was petite, had a face like something out of an anime—big eyes, small nose, a bit of mischief in even her most innocent grin—and though she looked Asian enough to be exotic, she was American enough to pass muster with even the most xenophobic father in her colorless town.

Her brother Adam, on the other hand, looked like a miniature version of the wide-faced, narrow-eyed interlopers the men in Chelmsford were certain were stealing their jobs. Or their tax money, by way of leeching off the government. Or their wallets, when they couldn't avoid driving under the bridge and venturing into the neighboring city of Lowell for something.

For a long time, Adam did his best to blend in. He stole the ads from the Sunday paper every week—and not the ads for the toy stores or the electronics places mind you, but the ads for the clothing stores, which is why his father worried about him for so long. *Worried* about him.

For all the wrong reasons, it turned out.

Adam stole those ads and he studied what the male models were wearing. He circled what he wanted each week, handed the ad to his mother (because she did the shopping), and then waited a week to do it all over again. Again and again, until he looked like a J. Crew model every time he stepped out of the house.

Except for the face, of course. He couldn't hide that. Not unless he started wearing oversized hoodies and enormous sunglasses. Not unless he contented himself to look like one of the rap kids at school, or the skaters, or like some hoodlum who'd transferred over from Lowell after his parents scored enough scratch dealing drugs that they could afford a nicer place in a nicer town.

He didn't dress like that until everyone else did, until baggie jeans were just what you wore. Until they were the only kind of jeans that any store sold.

His mother told him for years, before she took off for good, that he should be proud of who he was. She told him that there was no shame in looking the way that he looked, in being the man he was born to be. Her father had been a handsome man, she said. And his father before him. Adam could've been the Joey Lawrence of Luzon, she said. The Mark-Paul Gosselaar of Manilla! Didn't he realize that? He was a good-looking boy. So, so handsome.

But he didn't listen. He didn't believe it. Not until Ashley told him.

༄

AND REALLY, the two of them getting together—Ashley and Adam—that was all Mrs. Gates.

One spring, in one of his last ditch efforts to keep his mail-order bride from shipping herself off to some higher bidder, Mr. Gates built Mrs. Gates a pool. And after years of watching Ashley hang at their house in a uniform of baggie sweatpants and even baggier sweatshirts, Mrs. Gates' jaw dropped when Ash stripped down to her bathing suit to go swimming.

"Why?" she said, gathering up Ashley's discarded clothes and shaking them in her general direction. "Why are you hiding all of *that* under all of *this*?"

Adam was just coming out of the house when all this happened, his eyes glued to his Game Boy. But he didn't stay distracted for long. When his mother saw what he was looking at, and what he *wasn't* looking at, she slapped at his bare chest with the back of her hand. "Have you seen this girl?" Mrs. Gates asked her son.

"I see her almost every day," he said, oblivious.

And that was when his mother, annoyed at his obliviousness, grabbed Adam by the chin and made him look. "Yes," she said, "but have you *seen* her?"

"Mom," Robin told her, nudging her with a hip. "Leave him alone."

Mrs. Gates let go of Adam, then she looked at her daughter. She squinted her eyes and *examined* Robin, from head to toe. Then again, from toe to head. Ashley was already in the water, and Adam was running to join her, and Robin didn't understand why she had to stay put. But she did, even if she didn't like it.

"Can I go now?" she asked her mother.

"He needs to spend more time with her," she told Robin, nodding. Her eyes were still narrowed, the clenched flesh at the bridge of her nose the only wrinkle to be found on her otherwise flawless face. "Yes," she said. "More time for him, less time for you."

"But why?" Robin asked. "Ashley's *my* friend."

"No," she said. "Unless your brother wises up and takes her for his own, Ashley's not your friend anymore. That girl," she said, and she shook a finger at Ashley—who was looking all kinds of cute in a two-piece that was almost a one-piece but not quite— "Now that girl is your competition."

3

Years passed, as years do, and Mrs. Gates grew tired of waiting for her son—The Oblivious Gentleman—to make the move that Ashley so obviously wanted him to make. So one night, while the two teenagers were sitting around the TV and playing games on the Nintendo, Mrs. Gates rolled them a joint.

Ashley reached hungrily for the blunt, as in love with her boyfriend's cool mom as she was in love with the boyfriend himself—maybe even a little bit more—and she Bogarted that thing for a solid minute before she passed it on. Of course, when she passed it to Adam, he hesitated so long she almost took it back. But his mother reassured him he wasn't going to get grounded, so he did finally partake.

Mrs. Gates said nothing about how at ease they both seemed with the activity, no "I guess this isn't your first time" joke or nothing. She just took her hit each time the joint came her way, then passed it on.

Soon enough, they were debating about where the game they'd been playing—*Where in Time is Carmen Sandiego*—ranked in the whole of the Carmen Sandiego canon. And could Carmen

Sandiego ever compete with *Oregon Trail* in the hearts and minds of their generation? And, come to think of it, would there *ever* be a game as good as *Oregon Trail* again? Like, *ever*?

Soon after that, Mrs. Gates took a final toke and excused herself. "This old lady is tired," she said, "and tired of being a third wheel."

Adam asked his mother what she was talking about.

"Two beautiful young people," she said, standing up now, "who'd have their clothes off already if it weren't for a meddling mother."

"Ma!" said Adam, and he hid his face in his hands.

"No one else in the house," said Mrs. Gates, "except for you two and me. And if I'd just gone to bed an hour ago..."

"Ma!" said Adam again.

Ashley laughed and fell against him. Then she squeezed his knee and told his mother that she wouldn't have had the courage to take her clothes off if it hadn't been for the weed.

Mrs. Gates smiled at Ashley as she climbed the stairs. And she would have smiled at Adam too, but his head was still in his hands. He couldn't look at her. Even when Ashley tried to pinch his chin and turn his head and *make* him look. He just shooed her away. But she didn't budge. She stopped trying to move him sure, but she just wrapped her arms around him instead. Ashley wrapped her arms around him, and she squeezed.

"She's so weird," he said to her, once he'd heard his mother's bedroom door open and close.

"But she's so right," Ashley whispered into his ear. And then, trying hard to stifle a giggle, she nibbled at his ear lobe.

"What are you—?" he started to say, but then she found a spot on his neck that robbed him of words.

Ashley loosened her grip on him just enough that he could get an arm free. Then he wrapped that arm around her and rest his hand on the small of her back.

Her lips had traveled from the nape of his neck to the top

ridge of his collarbone before she realized that his hand hadn't moved an inch. So she paused to tell him it was okay, and that extra bit of permission seemed to be all he needed. Soon enough, his hand had roamed down inside the sweats she was wearing. Then he took hold of her bottom and squeezed—tentatively at first, then definitively—like he was laying claim to some undiscovered country.

But he took his time planting his flag, so to speak. It was nine minutes before they were naked, which might as well be *ninety* when you're fifteen, and another five before he was back from the bathroom with the condom.

And then, of course, Ashley almost ruined it—even though she was the girl and was already naked and looked like all that and a bag of chips. Because when Adam walked back into the living room, he already had the condom on, and it was red.

It was *red*, and she was stoned. And so, Ashley laughed. And as she laughed, she couldn't stop herself from saying "It looks like you fucked a balloon animal while you were away."

But then she saw how he was looking at her, and the giggles went away. Adam was looking at her the way he looked at that video where Janet Jackson marches through fluttering red curtains in the halter top and the choker and sings about what she'd do if he were her lover.

Adam was looking at Ashley like, in that moment, he wanted nothing more—or less—than what he saw in front of him. *Who* he saw. And who he saw in front of him wasn't Janet Jackson. It was Ashley Silver.

When he was done, when he dared to try and take away the gift he'd wrapped up and given to her, she held him tight with a part of herself she'd never guessed could be so strong. Because the feeling, though it wasn't entirely pleasant yet—maybe not even pleasant at all, at least not really—the feeling was so curious. And she didn't want to stop feeling it. Not yet.

✥

IT GOT BETTER, of course. Good enough that one day, as he was teasing her—tapping his dick against her clit like it was a doorbell that her body might answer—she wrapped her hand around the shaft and pulled him inside.

"Wait," he said. "Let me get a—"

But then she squeezed and he shut up. She did some quick math in her head—badly, as it turned out—and told him that there was nothing to worry about. After her cousin Veronica got pregnant while still in high school, Ashley's mother made quick work of re-explaining the menstrual cycle. And then explaining it again. And again. So Ashley thought she had that shit down to a science.

She didn't, of course.

But the feeling of him inside of her, nothing between his skin and her own, was enough to make her come. And when *he* came? When he came like a cannon firing on the ramparts of her cervix, a castle as yet unbreached by gods or men? Forget it. She surrendered right then and there and gave herself over to the feeling. For the *second* time that day. And, without realizing it, she opened her city's gates to his invaders.

They hadn't even needed a Trojan horse to sneak past her defenses. In fact, they'd done better without one.

✥

ASHLEY DIDN'T TELL her mother until a few weeks later. Mum had come to collect Ashley's laundry, a basket under one arm, and she caught sight of the pee stick and its plus sign before she spotted Ashley's hand between her legs.

Once daughter finished explaining to mother what had gone down, Mum had only one question.

"So," she said, "you masturbating just now—does that figure into the story somehow?"

"Yes," said Ashley. "I was trying to rewrite history." But then, before she could explain further, Ashley went to scratch her nose and was struck by the fact that she still hadn't washed her hands —that she could smell her *self* on herself. And if she could smell herself, then Mum could smell her too.

She didn't want Mum to smell her.

While Ashley washed her hands, Mum stood to one side of the bathroom doorway and waited. Ash was waiting too, waiting for Mum to go "Yeahbutwhat?" But she didn't. She didn't say a word. That was her M.O.

As Ashley toweled off, she told her mother that, in order to do what needed to be done, she needed a revisionist view on how she got pregnant.

"A revisionist view?" said Mum, and she raised an eyebrow.

"I've decided that I conceived immaculately." That's what Ashley told her. "I was about to cry out 'Oh God' to thank him for his troubles," she said. "But then you walked in."

Ashley thought it was pretty funny, but Mum didn't laugh.

"I don't want to ask for Adam's permission," Ashley told her.

"You don't have to," she said.

"But it's his, too," said Ashley, and she ducked her head.

Mum took Ashley's face in her hands and made her daughter look at her. And she looked deep into Ashley—into the very heart of her—and she said "It isn't anything yet. *It* is a bundle of cells. And it's in *your* body, not his."

IT WAS the third time in three years that Dr. Michaela Silver, a pediatrician, had to order a pregnancy test. The first was for her niece Veronica, the second for a girl in the same grade as her son Michael. And now, now it was her daughter.

The only difference between Ashley and the other two: she was putting an end to her accident. She said that out loud before they'd even drawn the blood from her arm.

"This is *not* happening," she said.

But the nurse doing the draw misunderstood her. She thought Ashley was in shock. She thought Ash just couldn't believe what had happened to her. To the nurse, a transplant from Lowell who'd raised three kids while putting herself through school, Ashley Silver was just another prissy little Chelmsford chick. The type of girl who sauntered into the city on a Saturday night to steal baby daddies from hard-working homegirls. The kind of girl who bought a guy drink after drink on her own daddy's dime. The type who swore her affluence was an effective form of contraception.

The nurse thought Ashley was in shock—a poor, pretty little thing—so she tried to sprinkle a little sympathy on top of her sneer, and into the squeeze she gave the bicep where she'd soon pinch Ash with the needle. "It's okay," she said. "It *does* happen sometimes. Sometimes," she said, "it just *happens*."

Ashley never told anyone this, but the moment she realized just how much she loved her mother was when Mum rolled her eyes at the nurse and left her contribution to the conversation at that. Mum stood in the corner, and she didn't say a word. Not a one. When it was time for an eye roll, she didn't hesitate to commiserate. But otherwise she let her daughter fend for herself.

"Do you know what you'll do?" asked the nurse, still not getting it. She looked first at Ashley and then at Mum. And when neither of them said a word, she added: "If, well, *y'know?*"

Even then, Mum didn't say anything at first. She just stood there stone-faced, like she'd had a staring contest with Medusa and lost.

"Sorry," said the nurse.

"As Ashley has already said, this isn't happening."

The nurse nodded. "Right," she said. And Ashley saw the woman roll her eyes as they confirmed her worst suspicions.

Mum gave the nurse a nod. "Thank you, Stelle," she said. "Now, so that we can be done with this, could you please draw the goddamn blood?"

৩৯৯

ON THEIR WAY to the clinic, Mum asked Ashley: "If you don't mind sharing, was it at least good?"

Ashley nodded and said "Best time yet."

Mum nodded in reply, her eyes focused on the road ahead of them. But Ashley's eyes were trained on her mother. She was investigating every wrinkle on Mum's face—though there still weren't many, even as she approached 40—and she was watching every twitch of every little muscle. Ashley wanted to see what she could get out of her mother, if she could get more than most just by trying a bit harder.

But she couldn't. Ashley couldn't tell if Mum had caught that Ash was telling her, in not so many words, that the sex which got her pregnant was *not* the first sex she'd ever had. And if Mum *had* caught it, Ashley certainly couldn't tell how Mum felt about what she'd caught.

"And," said Mum, "did you—?"

Ashley held up two fingers and smiled. But when Mum didn't say anything, Ash thought maybe she'd missed the gesture because she was too busy driving. So Ash repeated herself. Aloud this time. "Twice," she said.

Mum smiled now. Big and broad and unmistakable. And *there* were the wrinkles, the crow's feet. Only they didn't make her look older. Just *wiser*. Because, along with that smile she'd smiled thousands of times in her lifetime—along with that gesture came another that Ashley couldn't recall ever seeing her mother make. In that moment, Mum did something so girlish and young that

Ashley swore she'd traveled in time and was no longer looking at the wizened doctor that Mum was today. In that moment, Ashley swore she was looking instead at the pre-med student who'd wooed her father all the way back in 1975, when he was selling peanuts at Fenway to pay his way through college. Mum, in that moment after Ashley told her she'd come twice in one round of lovemaking, she held a thumb to her mouth and bit down gently on the tip of that digit and on her lower lip. When she hit a red light, she turned to her daughter and repeated the word Ash had said. Just to be sure.

"Yes, Mum," Ashley told her. "Twice."

The light went green as she shook her head—still smiling, of course. She put both hands on the wheel and put them back in motion.

There was a minute of silence. Then a minute more. Then mother asked daughter: "What's your secret?"

Ashley laughed. Then she said, as both a declarative and an imperative: "Practice, Mum. Practice."

4

Adam and Robin Gates were raised Catholic. But, whereas the only trinket of their faith that Robin carried with her beyond her confirmation was the shame, Adam was a believer. So, when he got a call from the pay phone outside the clinic to tell him his girlfriend had just arrived—a call from someone he went to church with, someone who'd once seen Adam and Ashley walking hand-in-hand past their church on Middlesex Street—when Adam got that call, he was most unpleased.

He was standing amongst the protestors when Ashley and her mother walked out. And when he broke from the crowd to come for them, the first thing Mum said—before she realized who it was—was that he wasn't allowed to do that. "They're required by law to keep their distance," she said.

But then she saw that it was Adam and she uttered a simple, single "Shit."

"What right do you have?!" he shouted at them, as Mum hurried her daughter toward the car.

Adam tried to get close to Ashley, but Mum kept her body between the two of them. And the arm she didn't have around her daughter to hold the girl upright—she kept that free arm outstretched, as if to warn Adam to keep his distance.

"It was mine, too!" he shouted, once Mum had leaned Ashley up against the car.

She fumbled with her keys, then dropped them. And it was as she bent over to collect them from the pavement that Adam made his move.

He stepped around her and grabbed Ashley by the wrists. Then he gave her a shake. One, and then another. "Why didn't you tell me?" he shouted, so loud and so close that Ashley couldn't hear the next few words he said. Not at all. She had to close her eyes because the sound of his voice was just too much.

And because she couldn't bear to look at the tears in his eyes.

But whatever he said, and no matter how hard he was crying, the fact that he'd touched Ashley was the last straw for Mum. When Ash opened her eyes, the first thing she saw was her mother shove Adam away.

The next thing Ashley saw, a little ways away, was the door of another car open. Adam's father's car.

"Doc!" shouted Mr. Gates to Mum, as he hurried to join the fray. "That's enough."

Adam retreated behind his father, but he looked terrified just the same. He wasn't sure his old man could stop the wrath of Ashley's old lady. Mr. Gates didn't look too sure himself. His booming baritone might've intimidated a lot of people in their town—that, and the gun they all feared he kept in his glovebox as a matter of professional necessity—but Ashley's mother didn't flinch.

Mum shook the pointy end of a car key at Mr. Gates and told him to keep his son away from her daughter.

He nodded. "Absolutely," he said. "But it goes both ways, Doc."

Mum looked incredulous, like she might stab his eyes out with the key. "What does?" she said.

"You want me to keep my son away from your daughter," he said. "Fine. But you need to keep your daughter away from my son."

And it was those words that seemed to make something click inside both Adam and Ashley. Because they looked across the way at each other right then, from over the shoulders of the parents who stood their ground to protect them, and they said to each other with their eyes that they didn't want to be kept apart. Not forever, at least. Adam was mad. And Ashley would've been too, had she had the strength just then to do anything more than keep breathing. But they didn't *hate* each other. Not yet.

"Dad," Adam began, and there was a pleading tone in his voice.

"In the car," is all that Mr. Gates had left to say.

AND SO, compelled by their parents, Ashley Silver and Adam Gates stopped seeing each other. Which meant that, aside from passing each other in the halls at school, Ashley stopped seeing Robin as well. And that blew goats, since Robin was the best friend that Ashley had. One of the only friends, in fact.

But strict enforcement of the Silver-Gates Accords of 1994 didn't last long. They couldn't. Not when the other Silver and the other Gates finally met, after years spent like ships passing in the night. When Michael met Robin, when they became *Michael and Robin*, nothing would be the same again.

SIX MONTHS LATER, after years of nothing but fire *drills*, their school had its first honest-to-goodness fire *alarm* in like a decade.

It was Senior Week. Michael was off campus doing senior things, but Robin and Ashley and Adam were still in school when it happened. They were in the library, sitting on the floor amongst the stacks. And they were *supposed* to be studying for finals, but all Robin could talk about was the dance. The *prom*.

Yep. The once and future Punk Rock Goddess was all about what she was going to wear to prom, and what kind of corsage Michael would buy her, and whether or not she should've trusted him to pick out his own tux. Then she was on about how, even if this year's prom was shit, she still had next year too—her own prom—and her boyfriend would be a college guy then, and blah, blah, blah.

But then, in an act of mercy—mercy for Ashley, at least—some junior pyromaniac decided the demonstrate their prowess right there in the middle of the school day, and they were all sent home. Robin got in her car to go find Michael. And Ashley went off with Adam.

The first thing they did when they got back to his house was sneak into his sister's room. Adam wanted to show Ashley something, but he wouldn't say what.

The walls were lined with posters of Pearl Jam and Green Day and Sarah McLachlan. The floor was littered with concert tees, blue jeans, bras, and a towering pile of underpants. Two guitar cases leaned against her amp and an incense burner sat atop the nightstand. Beside that there was a framed photograph.

Ashley picked it up for examination.

It was a shot from that year's talent show, of Robin and Michael on stage with their new band. The two of them were huddled together, in the middle of their set, and singing into a single microphone. Smiles cracked through the veneer of their serious rock and roll faces, betraying the good time they were actually having. *Unironically* having. The photo didn't capture this, but Ashley had seen—from her seat in the front row that night—that the couple had kissed as the lights went down.

Ashley and Adam had been first in line to get into the show, just so that they could be front row to witness the spectacular collapse of their siblings' band in front of the entire school. That the kiss was what they got instead, the kiss amidst a roar of their schoolmates and a chant of "Encore!"—that was just too much. Rather than watch the rest of the show, they traipsed out back and into the woods to party with the stoners.

Setting the picture down on Robin's nightstand, Ashley told Adam, "In the car, on our trips down the Cape, Michael used to sing along with the radio. And, like, I'd punch him for it. Because back then he sucked. Like for-real sucked." Ash sighed. "But he just kept singing."

The old metal of the closet doors creaked behind her as Adam pulled them open.

"First," he said, as he pulled the prom dress into the light, "I can't believe she even agreed to go to the prom. And second, I can't believe she's going to wear *this*."

Ashley gawked at the dress, clenching her teeth to keep her jaw from falling. It was just as Robin had described it by phone: full-length and sparkly all the way from the spaghetti straps down to the hem of the skirt. But it was *tiny*. It was going to fit her like a glove, and she would look stunning in it, but Ashley couldn't see her friend ever leaving her room in it—in just *that*. Robin was too insecure.

Not that she should have been, at least not in Ashley's humble opinion.

The dress's particular shade of sapphire would bring out all of the subtle flecks of color in Robin's hazel eyes: the greens and the golds and the little bits of blue. Ashley stood there in her friend's room and imagined Robin's spiky hair slicked down, sophisticated, a jewel-studded clip on each side of her face. She'd wear some sort of necklace or something. Ashley could see it now. And maybe just one pair of earrings—dangly ones, sparkling in the low light of the dance hall—instead of the over-ornamented lobes of yore.

Ash imagined how big her brother would smile with Robin on

his arm as he climbed the grand staircase of the Park Plaza. She saw the two of them waltzing across the floor of the ballroom like they were the only couple there, like they were the prince and princess at the end of some Disney movie and the orchestra was swelling as the scene dissolved into the two simple words of "The End." And then she saw beyond the end. She saw Robin's dress balled up on the floor of a bedroom down the Cape, balled up alongside Michael's wrinkled tuxedo. She saw the two of them waking up together as the sun rose outside their window, its rays glistening across the purply blue of the morning tides.

Adam asked Ashley if she thought the dress was as lame as he thought it was.

"Totally not her style," said Ashley, lying. And then, because it looked like he wasn't going to let it rest until she agreed with him explicitly, she said "Lame, yes. So. Lame."

He closed the closet and held out a hand for her to take, then nodded toward the hall—toward the door to the basement, really —and he asked, "Shall we?"

❧

THOUGH THE BASEMENT WAS FINISHED, it still had the feel of a dungeon. Adam's parents had given him free rein down there once he complained about all the money they'd invested in Robin's guitars and amplifiers and such, but three of the four walls were still just the exposed stone of the foundation. The fourth, however—the fourth they'd hired Ashley's brother to paint a backdrop on. It was his first commission, and he did himself proud. It looked like the great hall of some venerable old kingdom, like something off the cover of an old D&D book. And Adam took great care to light the place in a way that only heightened the effect that Michael had been going for. Electric lamps were not allowed, only candles. And the grander and more elaborate the candelabrum, the better.

There were bookshelves stocked with stone gargoyles and dusty old tomes, too. But the center piece, the *pièce de résistance*, was this wooden throne that Ashley and Adam had stolen from the theatre guild's props closet while working crew.

That's where Adam sat while Ashley sucked him off. That's where he sat—King Adam, the first of his name—as his ex-girlfriend knelt before him and payed homage to the stiffening scepter of his cock, as she offered up the gift of her mouth and her deep, deep throat.

But Ashley had been the one to suggest this, as it turned out. So she felt she had only herself to blame.

They'd been eating Pizza Rolls and channel surfing on the day this new phase of their relationship began, but all they could find on the TV was coverage of the bombing in Oklahoma. Shot after shot of twisted metal and concrete. They kept seeing it, that whole place looking like an open wound in the earth, and each time they clicked away a little bit slower. But then Ash was clicking again, and they were deep into the channels his family didn't pay for, the ones that came in only because of the black boxes their fathers bought from shady corners of the Westford flea market (and only then if you hammered the right button the right number of times). And then, suddenly, Ashley stopped clicking, and the two of them caught a murky glimpse of two bodies grinding against each other.

"Oh my stars and garters," said Ashley, feigning embarrassment and holding a hand to her mouth. She asked Adam "What, pray tell, is that?"

Sheepishly, he took the controller from her and tapped the magic button. With each tap, the screen grew less wavy, less blurry, until the picture was crystal clear. And then they just sat there for a minute and stared, stared at the screen as a buxom blonde bounced on top of some thin, emaciated guy covered in too many tattoos. She faced away from him, toward the camera, and her eyes looked as lifeless as her huge breasts, which hardly moved despite her exertions.

"This is fucked up," Adam said, as he shuffled about in his throne, trying to hide his erection. "I shouldn't be watching this with you," he'd said. "I mean: not after everything that's happened."

But when Ashley pushed her hands up along his legs, when she unbuttoned his pants and unzipped his fly, he stopped complaining. On screen, they cut to a different shot, this one of the girl on her knees, her head tilted upward. Eyes closed, mouth open, and tongue out—she waited. Her stick figure of a man held her in place by the forehead, his dick aimed at her face like a cannon, and he worked himself with his free hand like he was trying to light a fuse with the friction.

It looked ridiculous, honestly, so Ashley turned away. She turned away and took Adam into her mouth again, for the first time in forever.

He smiled down on her from his seat in the throne, like some benevolent god, and Ashley dared to hope it was just the beginning. The beginning of them picking up where they'd left off. She hoped that he would soon bless her with the gift of his own mouth, just as he had once upon a time.

But that day hadn't been the beginning of anything. Except maybe the beginning of the end.

Because here she was again, with her head between his legs.

Ashley's reached with her lips for the base of his shaft, because the only way she could do this anymore was to imagine that she was trying to beat her own high score. If she could get just *a bit* further before the gush of his seed signaled it was GAME OVER, then *that* would feel like a victory. Then again, even if she did beat this level, there was naught but a glitch waiting for her on the end screen. They'd reached the limits of their new eight-bit relationship, and they could go no further.

Of course, Adam didn't think about it that way. He was always going for more. Always going for broke. He wrapped his hands around the back of Ashley's head and pulled her face further into the tangled black forest of his crotch. She gagged as she tried to push away from him, to push out from underneath his grip. But he wouldn't let go. He maybe didn't even notice she was struggling.

So Ashley bit the bastard. Just a little, but a bite for sure. And then, *finally*, he let go.

He winced and screeched "Ow!" as she fell backward away from him.

And as she got to her feet, Ashley told him he'd been hurting her.

"I'm sorry," he said, cradling his cock now. "I didn't know. It felt good."

"How about this?" she said to him, eyes on his junk to see if she'd left a mark. "You want to feel good? Make me feel good first."

He ducked his head, like he couldn't look at her as he said "I'm not ready for that."

"Not ready?" she asked him.

"No," he said, and now for some reason he could look at her. "Because," he said, "we know where it leads."

"And where's that?" Ashley asked him, playing dumb—wanting to see what he'd say next.

"It leads to a choice," he said, "that's really no choice at all."

Ashley turned away from him then, because she couldn't look at him anymore. If she had to look at him right then, she was going to slug him.

"Ashley," he said, putting a hand on her shoulder, trying to turn her—trying to *make* her look. To make her *see*. And that was too much. She wasn't going to be turned. Not by him, at least.

So she swung around on her own, and swung a fist right into his stupid face.

He fell to the floor, hand rubbing at that pretty chin of his, and Ashley looked down at him one last time before she left. His pants were still around his ankles, and his now-flaccid cock was limp against his leg. And—she squinted just to be sure—there were teeth marks.

Ashley smiled at the mark she'd made—the boldest mark she'd yet made on this unyielding and forgetful world—then she walked away and left him lying half-naked on the floor.

The Silvers had a house down on Cape Cod, and Robin's favorite place in the old cottage was the play room on the second floor. She and Michael had shared a lot of moments in that room, even just six months into their relationship. And so, even though there were two free bedrooms for them on the night after Michael's prom, it was the playroom where they slept.

Michael had asked his cousin Matt to set up an old brass bed for them in there, and to light the candles, and to load the six disc changer with all of Robin's favorites so that it could shuffle all night long. And when Robin woke up the next morning, it was just as perfect as he'd planned it to be—right down to the orange sun rising above the purple tides, a sky so beautiful that it might've been painted there by this boyfriend who always went above and beyond.

But Michael didn't wake up with her. No, he slept on instead. And though Robin did entertain the notion of curling up against him again and closing her eyes, the magic of the sunrise was too potent. Even after it was done and gone, she felt too alive to go back to sleep. So Robin took to looking around the room, to studying it from beneath the warmth of their covers. And one of the things she kept coming back to was the old mirror that the Silvers kept in the corner and kept covered with a sheet.

She'd asked Michael about it a hundred times at this point. And though he had a dozen different tall tales to keep her from peeking beneath the heavy cloth, she'd always tease him anyway. She'd grab a corner of the sheet, pinch it between her fingers, and threaten to let loose the horrors underneath. And he'd laugh at first, like the whole thing was just a lark and he didn't care if she just went ahead and did it. But then Robin *would* start lifting it. And she wouldn't have moved the thing more than smidge before he had his arms around her and was wrestling her back toward the couch while she giggled maniacally.

It was actually a pretty solid move. If Robin was feeling frisky and he wasn't, she just teased him about the mirror until he was on top of her again. Worked every time.

But on the morning after the prom, he was out like a light. And Robin was bored. She could reach her guitar, but knew she'd wake him if she started with that. And though she should have been studying for finals—she was only a junior, after all, and still had two weeks left of school—she'd forgotten her backpack at home in the rush to get ready. So Robin found herself staring at the mirror instead. Or, well, at the sheet the Silvers had draped over it however many years before. And she found herself thinking: what could it hurt to take just a peek?

Michael and Robin, when they slept together—when they got to the *sleeping* part of sleeping together that is—they slept back to back. So there weren't any arms or legs to extricate herself from underneath. And so, it wasn't more than a few seconds between impulse and gratification. But when she tore the coverlet off that mirror and cast it aside, what waited for her was not the clarity one expects from a standard-issue looking glass. What was waiting for Robin wasn't really a mirror at all.

It was a frame that framed nothing—nothing but the back

wall of the play room that is. The glass of this looking glass was all gone.

Robin did a double-take, then a triple. She waved her hand in front of it, but no hand waved back. She waved again. Still nothing. Then finally, she reached her arm through the frame.

And that's when everything changed.

Though all she'd done was reach through the empty frame of a broken mirror, her arm felt more like she'd plunged it into an ice-fishing hole. And what the hell was that about?

Among Michael's many stories about the old thing, there was one in particular that came now to Robin's mind. "The first mirrors," Michael told her, "were just vessels of one sort or another that they filled with pools of dark, still water." And that's what this mirror had been, he claimed. One of his great-grandfather's seven wives was a witch, an honest-to-goodness conjurer of tricks, and she'd made this mirror by enchanting water she'd captured from the nearby river.

It might've been horseshit, like so many of Michael's tall tales, but only the Silver Family's unofficial historian would know for sure. And lucky for Robin, she was staying in his house.

So she got dressed and went downstairs to talk to him.

IT DIDN'T GO WELL. Before she'd even had a chance to broach the subject of the mirror and who it had once belonged to, Michael's cousin was on the warpath. Robin was a bad influence on Michael, he said. She brought out the worst in him and amplified it. Michael, he said, needed a partner who reminded him to be silly sometimes, to take a chance on smiling that awkward beautiful smile of his every once in a while. What Michael *didn't* need, Matt said, was black fingernails or songs about God being dead.

Robin tried to get a word in, but Matt ended things by

bringing up what'd happened between Adam and Ashley. And just before he stormed out of his own kitchen to get away from her, Matt Silver promised Robin that if her family hurt his one more time, then they'd all regret it.

She stood there stunned—stunned, but feigning strength— and said "Oooh, I'm shaking in my Chucks."

But the truth was that she *was* shaking in her Chucks. He was a tall dude, and *built*, and he could've put a hurting on her if he'd wanted to.

So, as soon as he stormed out, Robin stormed out too.

☙❧

SHE ENDED up in the barn, where the rest of family's oldest things were kept. The few heirlooms, that is, which had survived the fire in the 50s and the subsequent yard sale that Grampy Silver had held to fund the construction of his new house. It was a strange sight, really. Somebody—probably Matt, since he'd taken it upon himself to become the family's historian—had cataloged the belongings of his great-grandfather's seven wives. And each of them, it turned out, had a table or a shelf all to themselves.

It was on the witch's shelf that Robin found the journal.

It was small, dainty enough to hide inside an apron's pocket, but it was bound in a leather that felt too smooth to be cow's hide. Robin's mind went straight to work on which kind of animal the witch might've skinned to secure the magic of a spell book, but even her overactive imagination never got around to considering the list of ingredients she found on the last page of the tiny tome.

"The flesh of five stillborns," said Matt when he found Robin there, standing in front of the witch's shelf with her mouth agape. "You read it right," he said.

"That's," Robin started to say, but she couldn't find the words just then for what *that* was.

"Horrible?" he said. And when she nodded, he nodded back. "And that's not the worst of it."

As Robin thumbed through the pages, her arm still a bit numb from her experience with the mirror, she asked Matt if he thought that any the witch's magic was real.

"I don't know," he said. "But *Ada* thought it was real."

"Ada?" said Robin, the name ringing a bell.

"Yes," said Matt. "That was the witch's name. Ada Coffin, if you can believe that."

Robin snorted back a laugh.

"I know," said Matt, rolling his eyes. "Claimed she was half-Wampanoag. Don't know where the Coffin came in. Haven't turned up an answer yet, but I'm sure I will someday."

"I met an Ada once," said Robin. "Worked at the same bar as my mother when I was kid."

"Maybe it was the same one," said Matt. Then he widened his eyes and wiggled the fingers on each hand. Like he was trying to be creepy, like he trying to cast some spell.

"Not likely" she said, setting the book back on its shelf.

"I don't know," said Matt. "There's a potion in there that's supposed to allow the drinker to travel backwards in time and relive their past. And if that's possible, then who knows?"

For the first time in ages, Robin thought of the article she'd found at the bar way back then—that silly prank her brother played on her when she was 12. The silly prank she used to have nightmares about, before she decided it was just a prank. And suddenly, Robin wanted to ask Matt if there was anything in the journal about traveling *forward* in time.

But Matt carried on before she could get a word in.

"Haven't tried it yet," he said. "Not a lot in my own life that I care to relive. But there's a variation," he said, and his face lit up as he said it, "that's supposed to allow you to bring someone back from the dead. Or, well, the way that she puts it is that you're bringing them back to life. And she says there's a difference, though I can't figure out what the difference is supposed to be."

Robin was rubbing at her arm while he said all of this, trying to get the feeling back, but it was only now that he noticed.

"What's the matter with your arm?" he asked her.

"I pulled a Pippin," she said to him then, because his story about the mirror really being a palantír was another of the yarns Michael had spun for her about the old thing.

"The mirror?" he said to her, instantly catching her drift.

She nodded.

"Show me," he said.

⚜

MICHAEL WAS STILL ASLEEP when they crept upstairs. Which was great, of course, because Robin had forgotten to cover the mirror as she'd left.

"Where's the glass?" Matt asked her, as he ran his hands along the outside edges of the frame.

"Gone," she told him.

"You swept up?" he said.

"No," she told him. "The glass was already gone when I took the shroud off."

"And so," he said, turning to Robin and looking quite puzzled indeed, "what did you touch? The frame?" he said. "Because *I'm* not feeling anything."

"No," she said, "I did this."

And, without really thinking about it, Robin reached her other arm through the frame.

She withdrew it and it felt ice cold, even colder than it had when she'd put the first arm through. Cold enough that she doubled over from the pain. Maybe it was because she'd held her arm in there longer this time. Or maybe it was that, when it came to magic, each increase in audaciousness had a commensurate increase in cost. Whatever it was, it hurt like a son of a bitch the second time around.

It seemed to have no effect on Matt, though. He reached one arm through, and then the other, and then both at the same time. Then he shook his head and looked at Robin, and any trace of camaraderie they'd had in the barn—when curiosity had gotten the better of both of them cats at once—any shred of sympathy he'd had for her was gone.

"You're fucking with me," he said.

"No," she said, rubbing her hands together.

"Yeah," he said, nodding. "You and Michael broke this last night during your *exertions*, and now you're trying to play it off as—"

"I am *not* fucking with you!" she shouted at him, and she held up a hand that was so blue even he couldn't deny that something was up.

From behind them, on the squeaky old bed, they heard Michael mumble.

"We can't hear you," spat Matt.

Michael sat up and smiled that goofy smile of his, the one Matt swore Robin had robbed him of. And she was so glad to prove the prick wrong in one more way.

"What did you say?" Matt asked him after a moment, when Michael was still just sitting there smiling.

"What I *said*," said Michael, "is that she's not fucking with you"—and here he smiled even more broadly than before—"because she's too busy fucking with me." And then, channeling the Dice-Man himself—the comedian Andrew "Dice" Clay—Michael punctuated his terrible pun with an equally terrible "Oh!"

IN THE CAR on the way back home, Robin noodled with her guitar. And she noodled for far longer than she'd typically noodled, because the noodling that day was especially fine. Especially considering the fact that her fingers had felt like icicles not a couple of hours before. Even Michael noticed, and he'd taken to *not* noticing because of the amount of times she'd sworn she'd slug him if he paid her another compliment about her playing.

But after he'd finished telling her that her solo on the new tune was the best he'd ever heard it—after that, and the smile she gave him in return—Michael said the thing that creeped Robin out so much that she stopped playing and almost threw her axe out the window.

"I got a title for it," he said.

"For the new song?" she said.

"Yeah," he said. "It's got this crunch to it that reminds me of 'Reptile.' You know, the NIN song?"

"Yeah," she said, remembering all too well the moment she'd fallen for him on the night they'd seen that band, the night they'd danced together to that song.

"And you know, like everyone's always on about how you and David and I are like this fucking love triangle, and you're this, like, slut for playing the two of us against each other, which is of course an utterly misogynist take on—"

"Michael," she said, "the point?"

"Precious Whore," he said. "That's what we should call our song."

Robin hadn't thought of the obituary in years, had long since decided it was just a prank her brother had pulled on her. But now her boyfriend had said the name of the song she was supposed to become famous for. And what did that mean? What. Did. That. Mean?!

"Precious Whore," Michael repeated. Then he gave her a playful nudge to get her attention. "What do you think? Sounds like a hit song to me."

"Yeah," said Robin, managing a weak smile.

But it can't be, she thought. *I don't want it to be. I don't want to—*

"Are you crying?" asked Michael, and he turned towards her. "I didn't mean to... We don't have to call it..."

Robin nudged his chin with a closed fist. "Watch where you're going," she said. "Eyes on the road."

He did as he was told, but he kept mumbling about how sorry he was for having upset her.

"I'm not upset," she said. And then, to get him to stop being emotional so that she might get a chance to be emotional herself, she lied. "I'm just getting my period," she said.

"Oh," he said, nodding.

"That's all," she said, relieved that the trick had worked once again. And then, just to reassure him enough to send him off into one of his daydreams, she added "It's a great title. Why don't you brainstorm the rest of the lyrics?" she said. "I just want to veg for a bit, OK?"

He nodded, then he left her alone for the rest of the ride.

❦ II ❦
ANOTHER LONELY DAY
1995-1998

❧ 6 ❧

As Robin backed her Skylark out of its parking space, and the warm glow of the storefront windows began to fade, mounds of poorly plowed snow crunched beneath her wheels. On the car stereo, Robert Smith sang that it was the perfect day for letting go. And he sounded ridiculous, that mopey old man, imploring Robin and Ashley to "get happy!" But they *were* happy. And the song, as insincere as it sounded to Ashley's ears, made them happier still. So they sang along.

They sang, and they slurped at their Slush Puppies like they were going out of style.

But if Slush Puppies and the Cure were circles on a Venn diagram, there were only a few songs you could comfortably tuck into the narrow lip of that overlap. And so it wasn't long before Robin was turning down the radio for the good of the mood, the strains of a cyclical piano melody and the swirl of synthesized strings drowning beneath the roar of the car's heating vents.

"I'm glad we did this," said Robin, tapping her paper cup against Ashley's like they were grown-ass women clinking wine glasses at a bar and not just a pair of teenagers in a hand-me-down car. "It's like old times," she said. "I mean, you and I, we haven't really gotten together since me and Michael—"

"Since me and Adam," Ashley added, slurping hard at the drink to kill the bad taste that his name left in her mouth. "Why," asked Ashley, "did we ever bother with each other's brothers anyway? Why do you *still* bother? You've been together like what, a year now?"

"Three hundred and sixty days," she said with a smile. "But who's counting?" And when Ashley didn't say anything, when all that girl did was frown, Robin added: "Besides you, of course?"

"How do you stand it?" asked Ashley. "I mean: it's *Michael*."

Robin groaned. "You know," she said, "almost everything that you loathe about your brother is something I find endearing."

Ashley scoffed. "For instance?"

"For instance," she said, "I *love* that he's so malleable. An artist one minute, a singer the next—"

"Some," said Ashley, "might call that an inability to focus."

"Well, *some*," she said, "just don't get it."

Robin gunned it through the tangled intersection of Chelmsford Center, which was like taking your life into your own hands back in those days before Civilization came to town and demanded a set of traffic lights.

"You think," she said, "that Michael loving NIN only after you introduced them to him makes him a poser. But what it really means, in my mind, is that he was willing to cast aside his preconceived notions of what music *should* be in order to adapt and appreciate a new paradigm."

"What the hell is a paradigm?" asked Ashley, making fun of Robin for trying to sound more grown-up than she actually was, but also kinda curious. *What* was *a paradigm?* Ashley wondered.

Robin didn't answer.

"Fine," Ashley conceded. "But the fact that he gave up painting to join your little garage band—"

"We play in a basement," Robin interjected. Then, smirking, she said, "Thank you very much."

"Fine!" Ashley snapped. "Your little *basement* band. The fact that he gave up painting to join Gideon's fucking Bible—that's dumb. Because your demo tape is good," she conceded, annoyed at herself for making so many concessions, and annoyed that there were so many concessions to be made, "but it's not *that* good."

"The *Phoenix* begs to differ," said Robin, with a supercilious little smirk and a lilt in her voice to match.

Ashley groaned, annoyed at the facts of the case, but she pressed on as prosecutors must. "Michael has been painting since he was a little kid," she told her friend. "And then, just because you spent one night hanging all over him, telling him what a great singer he is—which he's *not*, by the way—I just think that's *dumb*. Wicked fucking dumb."

Robin giggled as she told Ashley "You're fun when you're angry." Then she slapped a hand on her friend's thigh and squeezed.

When Ashley squeezed Robin's hand in her own, when she said "Honey, you have no idea," she meant it in the way that friends mean that shit when they say it to each other. She meant it as a joke.

But when Robin took her eyes off the road for a second to look at Ashley, Ash saw clearly that Robin hadn't taken it as a joke. No. She'd taken it as an *invitation*

Ashley was right: Robin had no idea, but now she wanted to.

NOT UNLIKE ADAM'S CELLAR-CUM-DUNGEON, the band's basement was adorned with more than its fair share of candles. But that was where the similarities stopped. The depths of Adam's house were walled with somber gray brick. But here, in the sanctuary that David Johnson had built for his band, the plaster was painted a deep, rusty red—the kind of color you felt warm just looking at. And everywhere you looked, there were soft squashy things on which to sit. No matter where you sat, there was always at least one book within reach. Often three or four or more.

And CDs! God, there were hundreds of them, maybe thousands, all shelved neatly along the far wall. Anything you might want to listen to. *Anything*. Because it wasn't *just* that you could listen to anything you wanted. No, David took it a step further. He seemed somehow to know, to always just *know*, not only what you wanted to listen to, but also what you *needed* to hear.

But, despite all of this, no object in the room better epitomized David than the piece of yellowed parchment he'd procured that autumn from a store on Newbury Street that specialized in gargoyles and other gothic things. The parchment hung above his fireplace in an ornate Victorian frame. And scrawled across the ancient—or at least ancient-*looking*—paper? There was just a single word: "Forgive."

That really was all you needed to know about David. No matter what had been done to him, he was always ready to, as Grampy Silver used to say, "let bygones be bygones."

The band was the perfect example. Who among that motley crew would hesitate to poison the well of a friend when it suited them? Billy? Well, all boastful Billy Mills had done was to announce to a battle-of-the-bands crowd that had just awarded first place to some other quartet that the band didn't need the "stupid" prize money anyway, because he had just secured them, through his "connections" in Boston, a record contract of their very own. Oh, how the crowd had oohed and ahhed over that; David had lost count of how many people asked for details every day in the halls at school. But when David pressed Billy for details, both for himself and for the inquiring minds of Chelmsford High, all Billy could say was, "I'm working on it." A month later, "I'm still working on it." And two months after that, "Some-times shit falls through." Which was easy enough for Billy to say, because he had already graduated, because he didn't have to pass the sneering faces on his way into musical rehearsals; he didn't have to listen to whispers end abruptly whenever he entered the chorus room—that terrible, lonely silence.

Robin, with whom David had conceived this sonic gang of theirs—well her best Judas impression came in her steadfast refusal to side with David on any band-related issue, despite the supposedly heartfelt proclamation she had made to the contrary during their very first practice together. He had always wanted their fourth member to be a bass-player, which would have allowed him to stay on rhythm guitar and on lead vocals, and Robin had said she would back him on that "one-hundred percent." But when Michael came around, when he did whatever he did to get her juices flowing, and she invited him to join as their singer—Michael, who couldn't play any instrument at all—Robin had relegated David to the bass, to the role of sideman. And when Michael began to assert himself, when he suggested they play "Go Your Own Way" at the talent show—David scoff-ing, "The Fleetwood Mac song?"—who had Robin sided with then? Her boyfriend, of course, who had come up with what she called, "a brilliant idea," an idea that played off of the school's perception of their little love triangle.

"Nobody will get it," David had said. "You give them too much credit."

But Michael had sneered and said, "You don't give them enough."

Yes, David had surrounded himself with snakes, but Michael was the worst of all. Michael—fucking *Michael*—who had been with David the day he bought the hopeful bit of parchment which hung above the fireplace now.

Ashley had warned David, countless times, to break off his friendship with her brother. But he never listened. "It's only a matter of time," she told him once, adding up his stack of comics from behind the counter at the store where she worked now. "It's only a matter of time before he moves on to something else, or some*one*. He's like Forrest's box of chocolates," she said. "You never know when he's going to start sucking, but it's guaranteed that he'll suck eventually."

Michael had stolen the girl, and the band, and there was no telling what he'd pilfer next. And yet, David had forgiven him. He had forgiven them all.

Which was why it was into David's arms that Ashley had been fleeing the past few months. After all, if David could put out the fires of those burning bridges, if he could heal wounds which cut that deep, then perhaps, she'd reasoned, he could help heal her too. And sure, it hadn't been going exactly according to plan, but there was still... Time? Potential?

There was still something. And Ashley wasn't ready to give up just yet.

"You two together?" asked an unfamiliar voice.

"What?" Ashley stuttered, blushing. "No. No, we're not... not exactly."

"No," said the woman. "No, I suppose not. Too much fire in your eyes."

Ashley sipped water from a green Solo cup and cast a sidelong glance at her inquisitor. She was impossibly beautiful, the kind of woman not found in nature (or at least not in Massachusetts). Her flawless face was framed by a bouncy layered shag of cherry red hair, an obvious attempt—and a good one, it turned out—at 'the Rachel,' that ubiquitous haircut of the moment. She was dressed normally enough—a white turtleneck and skinny jeans accentu-ating her tall, lean frame. But her midriff, left bare by both the sweater and the pants, was preternaturally tanned and toned. The jeweled stud which pierced her navel looked more glitzy than any engagement ring Ashley had ever seen—Mum's included.

Suddenly aware that she was staring, Ashley turned her eyes

back to the heated band meeting spilling out from the cramped boiler room. "Are you with someone?" she asked the stranger.

"The drummer," said the woman. And then, with a definite question mark at the end of his name, she said, "Billy?"

Ashley smirked, everything clicking. Of course the woman was here with Billy. Billy, who had not gone to college, who had landed himself a cushy job at a computer company, who still lived at home, who had plenty of disposable income. Billy, the consumer. Of food, of video games, and now, apparently, of the world's oldest commodity.

"How'd you two meet?" Ashley asked.

"Mutual friend," she said.

"Benjamin?" Ashley offered with a smile.

"Yes," said the woman. "I think so."

"You *think*?"

She laughed. "I know a lot of Benjamins," she said. "It's hard to keep track."

"How many?" Ashley asked, wondering if she'd tell her.

She counted off on her fingers, and Ashley was so entranced by the sight of them—nails manicured to perfection, but in an understated way that seemed in direct opposition to the mandates of her profession—Ashley was so entranced that she had to ask the woman to repeat herself when she said "Eight."

Ash could feel her bottom lip drooping as she thought about that number. *What did you have to do for eight hundred a night?* She swallowed hard, then stuttered out her next question. "I guess," she said, "you don't have have to hold down a regular job with friends like that, huh?"

"Well," she said, "I also do some work over in Billerica." She looked casually over one shoulder and then the other, as if to assure they weren't being overheard. "I dance," she elaborated. "Great money if you know what you're doing," she said. "All about the tips, of course."

"Didn't they lose their liquor license?" Ashley asked. "I read that in the paper."

She nodded. "But they embraced it. They're 18+ now. Clientele's younger, which means they don't have as much to blow, but they're easier to please. And there's a lot of them. So I make it up in volume."

Ashley nodded along, as if she could relate. And it was as she was doing that, as she was nodding and smiling like a Stepford Wife on the fritz, that something weird happened:

The woman started to size Ashley up.

It took Ash a second to realize what the woman was doing, but then it was plain as day. "What?" said Ashley.

"Girl with a body like yours," she said, "could make a pretty penny."

Ashley rolled her eyes.

"You see that Jag out front?" asked the woman.

"Belongs to the dealers across the street," said Ashley, trying to sound certain of it though she was anything but.

The woman shook her head. "It's mine. And if I had a picture, I'd show you the lake house I have up on Winnipesaukee. Which I bought with cash. Up front."

"And if you hadn't just snorted it all out of the crack of Billy's ass, you'd share your blow with me too?"

The woman laughed, just a little. "You want more than money," she said. "I respect that."

"Well," said Ashley, trying to be witty, "it can't buy me love."

"Sure," said the woman, "but it can buy you just about anything else."

They stood silent again, staring across the room at the band arguing with each other in the boiler room. Trying to figure out what they were saying by reading lips. But the woman must've stopped staring first, because she was staring at Ashley again by the time she said what she said next.

"You wish you were one of them," she said, as if she were being paid for analysis and not anal.

And she might've been on to something, thought Ashley. *When your brother is an artist and the two cousins you grew up with are a writer and a musician respectively, isn't it natural to suffer from a bit of an inferiority complex?*

"Your beauty," said the woman. "Your beauty is your gift."

Ashley scoffed. "You sound like my mother."

"Maybe," she said. "But your mother and I, we have a point. And if he doesn't see that, if he doesn't appreciate the gift you're laying at his feet when you—"

"He actually doesn't like feet," Ashley told her. "It's a bit of a thing. I usually bestow my gifts in other places."

The woman laughed, but then she took gentle hold of Ashley's forearm. "If he doesn't appreciate what you've got on offer—if he's not *worthy* of it—then toss him aside."

Ashley looked the woman in the eye, then glanced down at the place where she'd been touched without asking. Then the woman withdrew her hand and blushed for the very first time. Ash could see her thinking that she should have known better. Her profession was all about boundaries, all about which ones she was comfortable pushing—and which ones her clients were comfortable pushing—and Ashley could tell that the woman prided herself on not guessing wrong. Or maybe on not guessing at all.

"Toss him aside?" said Ashley.

"Men are like Kleenex," she said. "Really. Pull one out of the box, use him for what he's worth, and then throw him away. When you're ready for another, guess what? There's always another one right there! They pop out of the box for women like us—fresh and clean and ready to do whatever you ask of them."

Ashley told her that was kind of obnoxious. And insensitive.

"The way girls like us are hurt by men," she said, "it's the only way to—"

"I haven't been," Ashley spat. "Hurt by men," she added, when the woman looked confused. "What makes you think—?"

The woman laughed, told Ashley that she was no enigma. She said Ashley wasn't nearly as mysterious as she thought she was, that nobody her age was. "I've been around the block," said the woman. "And you're like an open book to me, some old paperback I've curled up with a hundred times."

"You curl up with a lot of underage girls?" asked Ashley.

The woman rolled her eyes. "It was a metaphor."

"I'm surprised you can read," said Ashley.

The woman shook her head again. "The pages of you," she said, "are dog-eared and torn."

Ashley was about to tell the woman off once and for all—"if the pages of me are dog-eared and torn," Ashley wanted to say, "if I'm a worn-out page-turner, then what kind of book does that make you, you old bitch? You a Dead Sea Scroll, or something?"— Ashley was about to tell the woman off for good, and stomp off for good measure, but her rage was quelled by the weight of a hand on her shoulder. And by David's melodious voice in her ear.

"I'm sorry to interrupt," he said, smiling. "But if you want to have that talk, I have time now."

"What about the show?" Ashley asked, turning to face him.

"Well," he said, pausing for a deep breath, "your brother has finally consented to open with a Cure song—'10:15 Saturday Night,' actually—but only if we wait until precisely 10:15 to begin the show."

Ashley groaned.

"I'm sorry," he said, extending a hand to his girlfriend's antagonist, "but we've not yet been introduced, have we?"

"I'm here with Billy," she said, shaking David's hand. "I'm Nikki."

"Nice to meet you," said David.

"Yes," said Ashley, slipping her arm around David's to pull him away. "Very nice to meet you. But we're going to go now. Lots to chat about, you know."

"Oh, I'm sure," said Nikki, shooing them along with a knowing smile on her face. "You two have a nice talk."

ASHLEY PULLED HIM ALONG, zigging and zagging her way through the crowd and heading toward the stairs. And it wasn't until they were halfway up—and safely out of earshot—that she whispered to David that Billy's date was a prostitute.

David smirked. "An escort, actually."

As they crept out of the stairwell and into his kitchen, Ashley asked if there was a difference.

"A subtle but important one," he said. "According to Billy, at least. Sex is not mandated with an escort," David explained. "It may be implied, but it's not required."

"Huh?" said Ashley.

"Ostensibly," he said, "Billy's paying for a date. The theory is that, like any old date, the more riches he lavishes on his companion, the more willing she'll be to part with her virtue."

Ashley sighed and shook her head as they stole through the kitchen and into the living room. A cluster of their classmates huddled around the television, laughing hysterically. On the TV, a Japanese man was carrying a golden volleyball across a rickety rope bridge. And it swayed this way and that as he ran across it, as he dodged barrage after barrage of black balls rocketing his way from off-screen.

The balls, it turned out, were fired at him by a mob of militants armed with air cannons. And when one of the black balls hit the man on screen square in the crotch, the living room crowd exploded with cheers. The man dropped his golden parcel over the side of the bridge, then took a second hit—this one to his noggin—before falling off himself, down into the muddy pit below.

Ashley felt wrong laughing, but laugh she did. Then she asked David, who was smiling broadly, what it was they were watching. Because maybe she could tape it off him to watch at home, when she had far less pressing things to attend to.

"Takeshi's Castle," he said. "Japanese game show. Tyler brought it."

"Where does he find this stuff?"

David shrugged. "Don't know; didn't say. But that's Tyler for you. The only truly original person I've ever met."

On a night where it seemed that everyone she interacted with was going to do the best they could to piss Ashley off, this really took the cake. Not that she needed to be the *most* original person he'd ever met—she wasn't looking for a fucking prize, after all—but to be lumped in with some second class of poser plebes below the Almighty Tyler? That was too much. But she had well-laid plans, so she swallowed her pride.

Ashley nodded in the direction of David's bedroom and said, "We should go have that talk now."

David, still transfixed by Tyler's latest demonstration of originality, murmured something inaudible, almost as if to say "Can't we just stay here and watch this instead?" But he didn't protest when Ashley tugged on his arm again. What boy would? Because Ashley knew that, as much as a guy might have loved Japanese game shows—or *originality*, for that matter—there was always one thing he loved more.

But when it was over, it was all she could do to keep from crying.

She'd come so close she'd actually felt the last wave coming on, the big one, its shadow falling over her as it crested high above. But just like each of the other times with David, it was as if Adam was right there inside her head. It was as if he were *right there*, ready to pull her out of the water at the cruelest possible moment—just before the crash. And as he carried her to the shore, away from the sea Ashley so longed to return to, he whispered into her ear with a kind of faux Asian accent, a bad impression of his mother and her people, "None for you."

Could you be racist against your own race, Ashley wondered. Cause, if you could, the Adam in her head was.

Every time with David had ended liked this. It always ended with Ashley huddled beneath the covers—shivering, sheets pulled up to her chin—and with him standing at the foot of his bed, getting dressed, his bare chest pink with warmth, a positive glow about him.

That was my glow, Ashley thought. *MY warmth*. Which she'd given to him because she thought it would be an even trade, that she'd get his in return. But no.

David was haphazardly re-applying his eyeliner—in between glances at the wall clock—as he asked: "Did you intentionally prolong this particular talk, knowing that your brother would be pissed about the show not starting on time?"

Intentionally? thought Ashley. Well, no, not just for the sake of pissing her brother off. Her *intent* had been to come, however long that took. That was her *intent*. She wanted say "I'm sorry that my clit is not an on-off switch," but she didn't.

"Ash?" said David.

"Honestly," she told him, sitting up and starting to collect her clothes, "I try *not* to think about my brother when I'm having sex."

David grunted, squeezing a glob of hair product into the palm of his hand. "I beg to differ," he said. "If you aren't worried about your brother's perception of you, why all the euphemisms for our relationship?"

"I'm sorry," she said, anger flooding her with a sense of

warmth that the sex had not, "but was this"—she waved her arms over his tangled sheets for effect—"was this bad for you?"

In the mirror, Ashley could see him smile. But she also caught him rolling his eyes at her.

Ashley frowned at him. "Judging by the look on your face when I used my mouth to"—and here she made air quotes with her fingers, because fuck him for calling her out on *her* euphemisms when he had plenty of his own—"when I used my mouth to 'hide the evidence'," she said, "judging by the look on your face when I did *that*, I'd say—"

"It was fine," he said. "I'm not criticizing your sexual prowess."

"Well, good," she said. "Good. Cause I'm good in bed."

"Yes," he said, checking the final look of his hair before toweling the excess gel from his hands with a packet of Wet-Naps.

Ashley got out of bed and began to dress herself. "Billy's date," she began, "she was telling me that I could make it as a dancer."

"Well," he said, pausing for a few seconds before continuing. "There's a lot of training involved. Not that you're looking to become the next prima ballerina assoluta, or even just a garden-variety, non-assoluta prima, but most members of most reputable companies have been training since they were—"

"Stripping," Ashley clarified. "She thinks I could make it as an *exotic* dancer."

"Oh," he said, casting his gaze at the floor as all of his nonsense notions about her future flew out the window on a bumptious breeze.

"Why would an escort be talking to me about the ballet?"

David folded his arms, bit on his bottom lip, and bobbed his head to one side and then the other. He tapped his fingers on his arms. And then, abruptly, he unfolded his arms and began to tap his foot. He paced.

"What?" Ashley asked him. "What do you want to say?"

He stopped pacing, then raised a finger to his lips to shush her. Just then, outside the bedroom door, two raised voices argued their way closer and closer.

"We've got a show!" shouted Robin. "You can't just leave."

"We *had* a show," Michael shouted back. And then, almost as if he could see his sister and his one-time best friend through the door—could see where Ashley and David were hiding—his voice growled in their direction. "We had a show, but David had *things* to do."

Even though she couldn't *actually* see them, Ashley could see in her mind the air quotes her brother made with his fingers as he said that word. And in that moment she *hated* that they shared that affectation. She *hated* that Michael was her brother. And that he had just called her a "thing." As if she were no better than the blow-up doll that he and David bought on a lark and sometimes invited to the stage as a fifth member of the band, the one that David *swore* he'd never taken out of the band's basement. *Swore* he'd never used for its intended purpose. Ashley was like her now?! Little more than a repository into which this latter-day Order of Onanites could spill their seed?

"And now Billy's gone," said Michael.

"We can do a show without Billy," said Robin, laughing at how absurd it was that Michael couldn't fathom the disposability of drummers. "We'll just go acoustic," she said, "do a whole unplugged thing. You can grab a couple of bongos and bang out something simple."

"I've got things to do too," he said. "You know I was planning on heading down to Harwich tonight."

"Why?" she asked. "What the hell is down the Cape except for your queer cousin and that creepy old house?"

A door slammed open, and then another, and then there was more screaming. It passed through the hall, where it was muffled, and then out into the yard outside, where it grew clear again.

They were yelling about Michael's unrealistic standards as David finally twisted the doorknob and led Ashley out into the living room. The room had cleared, the crowd having followed the drama down the hall and out onto the porch.

On the TV, another man was knocked from another rope bridge by yet another crotch shot. But there was no one there to laugh at it. *And if a joke falls in a forest* thought Ashley, *and there's no one there to hear it, is it still funny? Is it still ORIGINAL?*

Ashley smirked at the thought. But she kept it to herself.

David snuck the two of them into the back of the throng, doing their best to blend in, and Ashley got a glimpse of the street corner just in time to see her brother's Ford Tempo racing off into the night.

Robin kicked at the chain link fence, then stormed her way through the crowd, right toward David and Ashley. The masses parted like the Red Sea before Noah or Jesus or whoever that was, and deposited Robin directly in front of the the two people who, based on the scowl on her face, she'd been longing to have a word with.

"You two have a nice chat?" she asked.

"Didn't quite finish," Ashley told her. "But them's the breaks."

And though Robin was still scowling, Ashley could see in her friend's eyes that she caught the euphemism. And that, on some level, she appreciated it. And felt bad for what it meant.

"You want to finish?" she said, and there was a hint of an invitation there in her own euphemism. A hint so subtle no dude would ever catch it. But Ashley could. She could tell that Robin was RSVPing to the invite she thought Ashley had been making earlier in the evening. She was RSVPing with an invitation of her own.

Ashley let herself get lost in her friend's eyes in that moment, in the beauty of them. And she imagined Robin's body next to hers, on top of hers. Beneath. In her head, Ashley wondered if there was such a thing as *too much* beauty, if two beauties might cancel each other out and make something ugly instead—or if one beautiful thing simply magnifies another. If you're careful not to get too obsessed with one or the other, that is.

Robin had regaled her time and again, often ignoring Ashley's protests that she stop, with tales of how she'd puzzled pleasure out of Ashley's perplexing brother. But now she could see how Robin might wander about the warren of *her* body, how the two of them might—to mondegreen the lyrics of the late, great Kurt Cobain—have themselves a breed.

Ashley was lost in Robin's eyes. But she was also just plain lost. And tired. And she said as much. And that ruined it.

"Okay," said Robin, and now she wouldn't look at Ashley anymore. "It's time for us to go anyway. You've got your learner's permit with you, right?"

Ashley told Robin that yeah, she did. "But why?"

Robin plunked the keys to her car right into the palm of Ashley's hand. "Why?" she said, and she scoffed. Wasn't it obvious? It wasn't obvious? "You're driving," she said. And then, surveying the crowd with squinted eyes, she pointed at Tyler. "And he's coming with."

"Show's canceled then?" David asked Robin.

"What do you think?" she shouted over her shoulder, leading Ashley and Tyler toward the street.

"Where are we going?" Ashley asked, unlocking the car.

"We're driving," said Robin, nearly shoving Tyler into the backseat before getting in beside him.

"Where?" asked Ashley.

"I don't care," Robin spat. "Anywhere but here."

"Are we dropping Tyler off?" asked Ashley.

"Ashley," she said, "would you just get in the fucking car?"

Obediently, she drove them out of the Highlands and back onto 110. And she did her best to ignore the sounds of zippers unzipping, of lips smacking against lips, of wet skin rubbing against tight vinyl. But it was hard.

Ashley also did her best not to laugh at how 'original' Tyler was when he had to beg Robin, after just *two* minutes, to stop for a second.

And she tried not to think about the fact that this was what she'd asked for, that this was what she had wanted. In theory, in her imagination, the fight was the end of it—the end of Michael and Robin.

But in practice? In practice, this was something quite different. Ashley saw, in her mind's eye, how Michael would react when he found out.

And how he might've reacted if he'd found out that it was *his sister* who Robin had taken to the back seat, and not poor Tyler.

Ashley remembered, all too well, what he looked like creeping out from under the couch where he'd hidden during their family's last game of hide and seek so many years before

She could see him creeping out from under the couch, after she'd bounced up and down on the thing to announce to their cousins that she'd found him. His face was black and blue, his eyes red, and his eyelids swollen with tears he refused to cry in front of anyone. Even when she'd poked him in the chest to try and make the tears come.

When Michael found out about Robin and Tyler, it'd be the same thing. He'd just stand there and take it. He'd take it like a man, whatever the hell that was supposed to mean. He'd save his tears for himself, for him and him alone to have and to hold. And *god*, how fucking annoying that was. How could he just stand there and *take* it? How?! From Robin, from the world...

From me? Ashley thought.

Because that was Michael's only crime against her, she realized at that moment. The only wrong that little bastard had ever done her was to exist, to stand strong and never crumble under the pressure she exerted upon him. Never even to *erode*, even after all the times she was like a maelstrom pounding at his shores.

In the back seat of Robin's Skylark, Robin and Tyler were back at it. And suddenly Ashley was back in her own body, and back behind the wheel.

They crossed beneath the Route 3 overpass, out of Lowell and into Chelmsford. And as they drove past the cinema and the Market Basket, Ashley seethed inside. She had no idea where she was going, or even what she was doing. So Ashley turned into the parking lot of the Chelmsford Mall, creeping slowly down the hill toward the strip of department stores.

When she reached the bottom of the hill, she started to do donuts in front of the Bradlees. One circle after another. Because it was the most ridiculous thing she could think of to do, and this was the most ridiculous situation she could think of to be in.

Why wasn't she in the car with her brother right now, heading down the Cape? Why wasn't she on her way toward something that mattered? Why was she here instead?

"Ashley?" Robin finally asked her. "What are you doing?"

Grimly, Ashley mumbled: "Waiting for the cops to show up."

"Well, shit," Robin groaned, zipping up one pair of pants and then another. "If you didn't want to come out with us, you could've said so. I would've just taken you home."

"Oh," Ashley sighed, pulling prematurely out of the last donut. "I didn't realize I had a choice."

She started up the hill again, swearing she would never use that excuse again.

"Hey," said Tyler. "It's past midnight."

"Yeah," said Robin. "So?"

In the rearview, Ashley could see him shrug as he said "Happy New Year, I guess?"

7

As far as Robin was concerned, 1996 was total shit.

She graduated high school and started at Berklee, sure. But her mother had left for good that spring, her band broke up that summer, and her boyfriend was so fed up with her wandering eye by Labor Day that he proposed an "Autumn of Anything Goes" so that she could get it out of her system.

And sure, the band got back together and skyrocketed to local fame. But that was on the back of the song around which her obituary would be written—so it was all downhill from there, wasn't it? And yeah, her mother sent post cards from places where she seemed a damn sight happier than she'd ever been at home. But that left Robin's dad so down in the dumps that he took up with his haggard ho-bag of a supplier, and as good as indentured his children to the woman. By October, Robin and Adam were spending whole weekends "working the weed" up at the ho-bag's place in the woods of New Hampshire.

There was a lake at Wanda's Weed World, though. So that was a plus. And there was a tree swing that looked out over the water.

Robin kissed so many people on that swing that fall, as the leaves of the maple it hung from fell all around them. Boys and girls and the first person she ever knew who used "they" as a pronoun. She kissed everyone who would let her, since she was allowed now to kiss anyone she wanted. Sometimes she was the one on the swing, and she'd lean back to peck whoever had just been giving her a push. And sometimes she would stand in front of the swing, at the water's edge, wagging a finger for some lucky so-and-so to come forth and lock lips.

Without knocking her into the lake, of course.

But that whole season, from equinox to solstice, Robin never once kissed the lips she was most longing to kiss. Because Ashley didn't care if it was the Autumn of Anything Goes. Anything and any *one* else could come and go, and many—*many*—came and went, but Ashley refused to be one of them. She wouldn't do that to her brother, she said. Not anymore. Ashley didn't like Michael any more than she had the year before, but she'd realized that she did *love* him. As annoying as that was.

That didn't stop Robin from trying, of course. If she couldn't get Ashley in on *her* act, as it were, she could still get Ash in on *the* act in general. And Robin figured that if she got Ashley to experiment a little with someone else first, if she got Ash through that trial, then maybe Ashley would re-assess her willingness to conduct some research on Robin after all.

It was Thanksgiving break when this debate between the two girls took its final turn.

They were standing in the corner of Wanda's basement and watching Michael and his friend Ian play Nintendo. The boys were blowing through extra lives like nobody's business, and Ashley was annoyed.

"Just because they uncovered the secret code—"

"That David played?" asked Robin, "And it pleased the Lord?"

It was a play on words to mock her friend and to calm her down, but Ashley gave Robin a look that said either 'Please don't' or 'I don't get the reference'—or maybe both—so she stopped.

"Just because," Ashley continued, "they've uncovered a way to get all the lives that they'll ever need..." But then she trailed off, and she grunted as she rolled her eyes. "Can't they at least *try* to attack the level with a little finesse?"

"How about you attack Ian with a little finesse?" said Robin. "And maybe the four of us can—"

"Ew!" said Ashley.

"Why 'ew'?"

Ash squinted at Robin and leaned close, and Robin felt like she was having her head examined. And when she didn't say anything, when she didn't catch Ashley's drift—when she couldn't smell the odor of Ashley's ew—Ash explained "Michael is my brother."

"I'm not asking you to do anything with Michael," said Robin, waving her hands.

"You're asking me to be in the same room with him while I'm having sex."

Robin nodded and smiled. "Yes. And while *he's* having sex. And then maybe we switch and—"

Ashley feigned gagging.

"No," said Robin, grabbing Ashley's arm to bring her back from the brink. "You come to me, and Ian goes to Michael."

Ashley looked back at the boys, at Michael clapping Ian on the thigh to congratulate him on completing the game, and she studied them for a minute as they traded war stories from their just-finished tour of duty. (As if they hadn't been sitting next to each other the whole time.)

"It would be fun," said Robin.

When Ashley looked back at her, she didn't look *entirely* unconvinced. But then Ashley raised an eyebrow and asked Robin if she thought Michael would be into that.

"It's the Autumn of Anything Goes!" she said. A bit too loudly, as it turned out, since Michael and Ian looked over at the two girls just after she said it.

"And what about Ian?" Ashley asked Robin in a whisper, covering the side of her mouth to prevent the reading of lips.

"He's a virgin," said Robin, mirroring her friend's gesture and decrease in volume. "His first year at college wasn't any kinder to his libido than his four years at CHS, and Michael tells me that the first couple months of this second year haven't been any kinder."

"Is it because he's fat?" asked Ashley.

"Would you sleep with him?"

"Yeah," she said. "He's cute. And fucking funny to boot."

Robin nodded. "It's not because he's fat," she said. "It's because he thinks that his fatness disqualifies him."

Now Ashley nodded. "And you think I should be the one to disabuse him of this notion?"

"Yes," said Robin. "And then give him over to Michael, so that I"—and here is where Robin took Ashley's hand and put the moves on—"so that I can disabuse you. Of some notions, that is."

Ashley looked back at the boys, who were staring at them now and probably wondering what they were whispering about. Then Ashley asked Robin if she thought that, just because Ian was a virgin, he'd really be willing to have sex with Michael.

"I think," said Robin, "that, at this point, he'd put his dick into any hole that would have it."

With her eyes on the boys again, Ashley told Robin—out of the corner of her mouth, in little more than a mumble—that she was game for the first part, but made no promises about the second.

Ashley made for the stairs then. "To get changed," she said. "I have just the thing to make him swoon." And though Robin tried to tell Ashley that he was already swooning, and there was only so much fun she could have with him if he passed out, Ashley wasn't listening. "It's like I was saying about the video game," she told Robin. "I already have everything I need to win, but why bother playing at all if you can't play with a bit of panache?"

"Where's she going?" Michael asked Robin, once his sister had disappeared.

Robin shrugged at him, then directed her attention at Ian. "I think she likes you."

Ian looked to either side of himself to see who Robin might be talking about, then he pointed at himself and let his jaw droop like codfish.

He wasn't the brightest bulb when it came to girls. Back before Michael, *just* before Michael—when Ian and Michael were seniors and Robin was a sophomore, Robin used to stop by Ian's locker every day on her way to English. He'd played Falstaff in the school's production of *The Merry Wives of Windsor* the previous year, and she'd been in love with him ever since. Talent-wise, he'd been so head-and-shoulders above the rest of the cast that Robin couldn't keep her eyes off him. And when she stopped by his locker each day of the fall of her sophomore year, begging him to audition for the next show—a musical—so that they'd have a chance to work together, it wasn't her eyes she couldn't keep off him anymore. It was her hands. Robin started giving him hugs every time she saw him. She started asking him for rides to school. When he asked Robin if her boyfriend at the time would be jealous of all the attention she was lavishing upon him, Robin told Ian that actors were sexier than violinists anyway.

But he still didn't get it. He didn't get that he could've gotten it, if he just *got* it and asked.

Robin sat with the boys on the couch while they all waited on Ashley, Ian and Robin taking turns battling Michael in Mortal Kombat. They took turns beating the shit out of him and his predictable pixelated schlub Scorpion, took turns doing the bidding of the voiceover guy in the game who demanded they "FINISH HIM!" at the end of each match, but all the while Robin was thinking about finishing Ashley. All the while Robin was thinking about cutting in on Ashley and Ian, like some asshole in some old timey flick trying to steal the hero's girl away.

If Michael had any moves in that game that his frantic tapping of the controller's buttons didn't give away, Robin might've been done for. But it was all too easy to beat on her boyfriend and lust about her best friend at the same time.

And then, all of a sudden, there were footfalls overhead. Ashley's footfalls. Robin nudged Michael, whose on-screen avatar was just then being beheaded by Ian's. Robin stood, in order to clarify her nudge, and when that didn't work she squeezed Michael's hand. But it was only after a long stretch of staring at the cartoonish gore on the television screen, at the blood dripping from the word FATALITY, that Michael finally clapped a hand on Ian's thigh and stood to leave.

"Where you guys going?" Ian asked, with a lump in his throat.

"We'll be back," Robin told him as she dragged her boyfriend away.

They passed Ashley on the stairs, Michael gawking as he asked his sister what on earth she was wearing.

"Is that mine?" Robin asked, and Ashley nodded.

"It doesn't fit," said Michael.

Ashley smirked at him and told him that was okay. "It won't be on for long." That's what she said as she honked his nose.

Years later, in recounting this event to Robin over drinks in New York—his star rising then on Broadway, and hers on MTV— Ian would explain that "out of all the naked feet and calves I've seen over the years, it's Ashley Silver's feet and calves coming down those stairs that I remember the clearest."

She was dressed in a black hip-length robe and a purple satin chemise, he said. And he couldn't stop staring at her legs, because he was too afraid of looking up at the bodice she was clearly spilling out of.

"Robin bought some new things for college," Ashley told him, crossing half the distance to the couch. "I asked if I could try them on."

Ian gulped, unable to decide if he was supposed to look her in the eye now or keep his gaze right where it was. "Is this something you girls do often?" he asked.

Instead of answering his question, Ashley began to untie the belt of the robe. And Ian watched her fingers while she did it. Suddenly her fingers seemed like a more innocent place to stare than her legs. But the way they worked, those fingers—pulling the knot out with just the faintest flick of her wrist—Ian... well, Ian thanked God that the couch was obscuring his crotch.

"What did you say?" he asked Ashley then, because he was sure she must've said something while he was off in La-La Land.

But Ashley just laughed and told him that she hadn't said anything.

"Sorry," he said as she removed the robe, as she let it slip to the cold, stone floor.

"What do you think?" she asked him as she rounded the couch.

He blushed and looked down, as much to will his damned erection into submission as to look away from the girl coming his way.

"Well," said Ashley, slipping her fingers under his chin to lift it up, "I'm not fluent in blushing. What does that shade of pink mean?"

"I think," he said, staring into the face she lowered to meet his, "that Robin put you up to this."

"Up to what?" she said, pressing his shoulders back into the embrace of the couch's cushions. "This?" she said, sliding one of her legs over his lap, her naked knee grazing the bulge in his jeans as she straddled him.

Now he didn't know where to look. His eyes were level with her chest, with the cleavage spilling out of the too-small chemise, but to look her in the eye seemed the wrong move too. He still hadn't looked her in the eye. Not really.

So he settled on turning his head to the right, looking off to the staircase from whence Ashley came.

Ashley full-on sat on his lap now, resting her bum on his crotch, her knees squeezing against his hips. She leaned in, brushing her cheek against his, a lock of her hair catching on his lips as she whispered to him, "Your body's saying what you're afraid to."

"What?" he said.

She took hold of his hands then, then put them on her knees. And when he didn't move them on his own, she took hold of them again and guided them up her legs, across her thighs, until his fingers brushed against the waistband of her panties.

"What are you afraid of?" she asked him.

"I..." he stuttered. "I've never—"

"I know," she said, her breath still hot against his neck, his ear. "Why do you think I'm here?"

Finally—*mercifully*—he took action. He squeezed her hips, which Ashley took as an invitation, and she RSVPed by pressing her lips against his neck. But she'd misread him. He was trying to get her off—not to 'get her off' in the Biblical sense, but get her off of his lap. Because he couldn't let this happen. He knew—he just *knew* that it wasn't real. And so, he pushed Ashley away and she relented.

As she fell back onto the other side of the couch, Ashley looked upon him with her eyebrows scrunched up and her mouth hanging open. But before she could say anything else—before she could apologize or explain—Ian stood up and ran for the stairs.

Robin was sitting upstairs, Michael passed out on her lap after one toke off a joint she'd rolled from Wanda's weed. She was sitting there, unfulfilled, reading an Anne McCaffrey novel. When they met up for drinks all those years later, Ian told her that every girl he knew in the mid-90s was reading Anne McCaffrey. Or Anne Rice. Or fucking *Anne of Green Gables*, for that matter. They just loved their Annes, he said. And Robin nodded, because she *did* love her Annes. They were always up to something. Or up *for* something. Like she was.

Maybe she should have been an Anne, instead of a Robin. That's what she was thinking as Ian raced by her and out onto the quiet country road.

"Hey," she shouted, a giggle in her voice as she extricated herself from under the heavy weight of her lightweight boyfriend.

But Ian ignored her and kept running. Sadly—for him, that is —he only made it about twenty feet before he was doubled over, hands on his knees. He was panting, about to retch, and he couldn't help but look at his crotch.

He was still hard.

Behind him, Robin's Chucks slapped against the pavement.

"Where are you going?" she said, putting a hand on his shoulder. "Jesus, Ian, you're going to give yourself a heart attack."

"If I die," he said, panting, "it's on you."

"How so?" she said. "Isn't Ashley the one who got you all hot and bothered?"

He stood up and glared at her. Part of Robin's charm, Ian told her later, was the mischievous glint in her eye. But when someone became the target of Robin Gates' mischief, he said, that was another story.

"Everything she did," he said to Robin, "she did on your orders."

She scoffed. "*Pshaw!*"

"You think she goes after the fat kid if you don't put her up to it?"

She poked him in the chest. "Haven't you heard not to look a gift horse in the mouth?" she asked him.

And now it was his turn to scoff. And he sure did. "You seem," he said, "to know an awful lot about Trojans."

Robin was about to say 'touché,' but right at that moment she heard something coming from behind her that stole her attention. Fully, and completely. And it was Ashley, the setting sun reflecting off the buttons on her leather jacket, which she'd thrown carelessly over the lingerie. She was stomping toward Robin and Ian in her bare feet, a scowl on her face.

"What the hell?" she said.

Robin nodded and gestured at Ian as she said "My thoughts exactly."

Years later, when he told this part of the story to Robin in that bar in New York, there was this look of pure admiration on his face. For Ashley, of course, not Robin. It was this wistful look, his eyes looking like he'd somehow traveled back in time to relive the moment. Like he'd made that journey to the past more times than he'd care to admit.

He'd been given every kind of sympathy known to man in his many years on this planet—from sympathy hugs to sympathy fucks—but this was the only time he'd ever turned it down. And, he told Robin at that bar in New York, he never did it again. The look that Ashley gave him, the looks that *both* girls gave him—their clenched eyebrows and drooping lower lips—are what he saw from then on, whenever he had the audacity to consider declining a kindness. Their looks, and what came next.

"No," said Ashley, turning on Robin. "I was asking *you* 'what the hell?', not him."

Robin tilted her head and put her hands on her hips. "Are you kidding me?"

Ashley shook her head.

Robin swore that she didn't know this was how it was going to turn out, but Ashley didn't believe her. She felt as coerced in that moment as Ian did. So she took his hand and led him back into the house.

LATER, as the last of the sun's dying light glistened across the lake, Robin caught the two of them out by the tree swing. They were sitting beside one another on the ground, Ashley's head on Ian's shoulder, and they each seemed to be staring at the swing. And though Robin didn't get close enough to hear what they were saying to each other then, Ian told her later what words Ashley spoke.

All of a sudden, Ashley sat up straight and turned Ian's face gently toward her own.

She told him that she would've said she was sorry. "But I'm done with regrets," Ashley said. "And so," she began to say, but then she stopped. She stopped speaking and she let her lips finish the sentence.

And Robin, she looked away. She looked to the swing instead, tried to see what Ashley had seen there, what she'd found so captivating. But all Robin saw was the empty seat.

An empty seat, swaying in the breeze.

8

Ashley's family was sitting at a table in Chef Mickey's when she told them. It was a few weeks before her eighteenth birthday, and she had just forked the ears off of a mouse-shaped waffle. Mum couldn't speak. Minnie—her favorite character—had just stopped at the table to say hello and pose for pictures in her polka-dot dress, and Mum must've been wondering if Minnie had overheard Ashley's announcement.

In an attempt to further fuck with everyone, Ashley asked "Cat got your tongue?"

At the sound of the word "cat," Minnie jumped in fright and covered her mouth with her gloved hands. She looked around in panic, searching for the cat. Then, after an exaggerated beat, "realizing" that Ashley was making a joke, Minnie wiped her brow with her forearm and feigned a sigh. Then she looked at Ashley reproachfully—or, well, as reproachfully as a person wearing a gigantic mouse mask on their head can look—and she wagged a finger. "What an awful trick," she would've said, if she'd been allowed to speak.

Ashley wanted to buy the person inside that mouse a drink. She decided that they *had* heard, that they were her age (and therefore sympathetic to her plight), and that they were now her co-conspirator. Maybe they'd had a similar talk with their own parents, not too long ago, when they'd confessed their desire to play a cartoon animal for a living. After all: how different was that from telling your parents you were going to start stripping? It was all about clothes, right. Putting them on, taking them off—what was the difference?

Mum glared at Ashley as each member of the family posed for a picture—glared right up until it was her turn, and then threw on a smile like it was no trouble at all.

As soon as Minnie moved on, Dad asked Ashley what she would call herself.

"What do you mean?" asked Mum. "What do you mean 'what will she call herself'?"

It was here that Michael chimed in. "Dancers never use their real names," he said.

Now Mum glared at *him*. "And how would you know that?" she asked him.

Michael looked down at his plate in shame. He de-eared his own waffle.

"I can't believe I'm having this conversation," said Mum. "Here," she said, gesturing wildly, "of all places."

Dad chuckled. "Mikki," he said, "if you think Ash didn't consider the location, then you don't know our daughter."

"Apparently not," said Mum.

Michael fidgeted like he was back on Alice's tea cup ride, the tension in the air like a centrifugal force slapping him from one side of his seat to the other. He hated confrontation. Ashley had counted on that, too. And soon enough, Mum noticed the plight of her eldest child and calmed herself down.

"Hannah," Ashley said, finally answering her father's question. "Hannah Hamilton."

"What?" said Mum.

"That's what I'm going to call myself," Ashley told her. "Hannah Hamilton."

Michael's eyebrows danced upward as he puckered his lips and screwed up his face in concentration. "I thought," he finally said. "I thought it was the name of your first pet, plus the street you grew up on?"

"Hannah High?" said Dad. Then he laughed. "Nah. She'd sound like she was straight out of a Cheech and Chong flick."

"You're using my maiden name?" Mum asked.

"And the name of my dog," Ashley said, nodding. "May she rest in peace."

"You're using my *maiden* name," said Mum, "for *this*?" She seemed equal parts annoyed and impressed by her daughter's dedication to this transgression.

"It's alliterative," Ashley told her. "It was either that or a double entendre."

"Chastity Night," said Dad.

"Cherry Johnson," said Michael, and he and Dad chortled in unison.

"Is this why you've been starving yourself?" asked Mum.

Ashley jabbed her fork in the direction of her plate and asked if anyone knew how many waffles she'd had that morning. When Mum said "No," Ashley told her. "Three," she said.

"Fine," said Mum, as Ashley crammed a forkful of waffle into her mouth. "But before vacation you were—"

"Ma!" Ashley growled, the detritus of Mickey's ear lobe spitting across the table as she did. Because, while Mum was Mum when they were getting along, Mum became *Ma!* when she fell out of favor.

"All that running," said Mum. "All those squats and crunches," she said, shaking her head. And then a thought grabbed her by the jaw and pulled on that thing until she looked like a codfish. "Is this," she began, "why I found the name of a plastic surgeon in the computer's search box?"

Dad looked like he was about to say something just then, like he was about to make a joke about Ashley writing off the new boobs as a business expense on her taxes, but Mum caught his eye and he caught his tongue. No cat necessary.

Mum shook her head, feeling stupid for not putting it all together before now. "Is this," she said, "why your body, which has always been good enough for you before now—and even *too* good sometimes..." She trailed off. "Is this what all that's about?"

Ashley had been waiting for this one. The table went quiet, even her obtuse-as-fuck brother realizing that shit was serious now.

She gave a quick sidelong glance to her right, and then to her left, just enough to make them think she gave two shits who overheard what she was about to say. Then she gave it to them straight in her best stage whisper.

"What it's all about," Ashley said, "is money." And then, trying to sound as convincing as Nikki had when she'd laid down this line nearly two years before, Ashley said: "And though money can't buy me love, it *can* buy me just about everything else."

"Like what?" asked Dad. But he didn't ask with even a drop of derision in his voice. He leaned forward and rest his chin on the half-crumbled steeple of his clasped hands, looking all kinds of curious. What *did* his daughter want out of life when she grew up? He couldn't remember the last time he'd asked. And seeing as she was about to turn eighteen, this might be the last time he *could*. Ask, that is.

"A house on the beach," she said. And when she saw them looking at her like she was little kid with nothing but clichés for dreams, she added: "With an arcade in the basement."

This addition seemed to satisfy them. So Ashley went on. "A car like my gramps used to make," is what she said next. "One to stand the test of time."

Michael nodded at this one, like his sister had stumbled upon something he longed for too.

"And vacations to anywhere I want to go," Ashley continued. "And to every place in this wide world that an uncultured white girl *should* see."

This one got Dad, who leaned back into his seat now and nodded as he did.

"And you're willing," said Mum, "to trade your body for these things?"

"Ma!" said Ashley. "Not my body. My *beauty*. This fleeting thing that'll go to waste otherwise. This thing that God gave me," she said, invoking the name of the deity that only Mum still believed in, "this thing that Michael is always trying to paint, that Veronica can't stop trying to turn into a song, that Matt can never find the words to describe—people *want* what I have, and they're willing to pay a pretty penny for just *a taste*."

"But I think," said Michael, leaning in and holding up an index finger—an affectation he clearly thought made him look more grown up, but which really just made him look like a cartoon—"I think what Mum is trying to say is that there are only so many licks until they get to the center of your Tootsie Pop, Ash. And then: what then?"

"The owl eats her!" said Dad with a laugh, slapping the table so hard that a spoon rattled off the edge and onto the floor.

"Well," said Ashley, "if it all ends with me getting eaten, I'm not going to complain."

They all went pink.

"Especially if I'm being eaten by a nerdy ol' owl who's done his homework."

And now they all ducked their heads.

"And do you remember the way he trilled his tongue as he said '*three*'?"

"Ashley!" said Mum, the first of them to come back to looking Ashley in the eye.

Ashley feigned a shiver of delight. "Ooh, I'm getting tingly just thinking about it. *Three*," she repeated, and she shivered again.

"And what about love?" said Mum.

"What about it?"

"You've acknowledged that money can't buy it," she said. "So congratulations on that. Your father's obsession with the Beatles has hammered at least *one* truism into your head."

"Okay," said Ashley, not sure yet where her mother was going with this.

"But here's something you may not have considered," Mum began. "What if the profession you've chosen, the one that's going to, as you put it, 'buy you everything else'—what if that profession ends up costing you more than you bargained for? What if it's not just that it can't *buy* you love, but that it will *cost* you love as well?"

Ashley rolled her eyes at her mother. "You think guys don't want to date strippers?"

"Date?" she said. "Maybe. Sleep with? Sure. But love? Marry?"

"Love," said Ashley, "is for liars and the lazy."

Dad and Michael looked up at the sound of this proclamation, as if trying to figure out which of those two options they were.

"Love," Ashley continued, "is a lie we feed little girls, a promise we make each night we crack open a story book and read them a fairy tale to put them to sleep. 'If you're good enough,' we tell them, 'and pretty enough,' then someone will love you. And once someone loves you, you get to live happily ever after. But what does that even mean, Ma? You notice how we never get to find out what 'happily ever after' consists of?"

"Sure," said Mum, shrugging and shaking her head. She'd already decided that Ashley's logic was flawed, and Ash realized she was a hair's breadth away from losing this battle she'd planned so long and hard to win. All those long hours around the round table in their kitchen back home while everyone else was off at work. Ashley, the queen of her kingdom, surrounded by bearded old advisors she'd plucked from her bin of He-Man and She-Ra figures—and that one skunk dude who smelled perpetually of patchouli oil. All the time she'd taken to lay out the pieces on the RISK board and consider what would happen if Mum made it past her defenses in Indonesia and New Guinea and cornered her in her Australian stronghold—was it all to have been for naught?

"We never get to see the 'happily ever after'," Ashley began, making a last stand, "because it doesn't exist. No one's ever seen it, so they've never been able to write it."

"Okay," said Mum. "So that's where the liars come in. But explain to me how love is for the lazy."

"The little girls we promise 'happily ever after' to—what they see when we say those words to them is a life where they no longer have to work at anything, where they can laze around for the rest of their days because of what their..."

And it was only here that Ashley trailed off. It was only here that she saw the corner she'd backed herself into. It was only here that she saw the size of the army at her gates—only here that the white flag at her feet began to feel like the only option.

"Go on," said Mum, and Ashley could see her mother was trying hard—*so* hard—not to smirk. Not to *gloat*. Mum held up a finger and spun it in a circle, as if the motion might jumpstart the stalled engine of her daughter's arrogance. "Because of what their...?"

"What their beauty has bought them," said Ashley, and now it was she who ducked her head.

"But," said Michael, trying to to be helpful, "she's not trying to buy love with her beauty. That's the *opposite* of what she's trying to do."

"Okay," said Mum. "But what does she do when she's bought everything she wants to buy? What does she do when the beauty's all been spent and she's left alone in her house with nothing but her video games and her antique car and her worn-out passport to keep her company?"

"She plays as many games of Ms. Pac-Man as she wants," said

Michael. "And she doesn't have to sit there and pretend not to be frustrated while she waits for some inept asshole she's dating to to finish his turn."

Ashley looked up from the table then, at the brother who somehow understood her better than anyone else, and wanted to give him a hug for maybe the first time in her life.

"Or," he said, having no idea how to interpret the look his sister had just given him, "you know, if you're in the mood to hang with an inept asshole at that particular moment then..."

"Then I'll call you," Ashley told him. "I don't need a boyfriend for that."

❦

THAT NIGHT at Disney's World Showcase, Dad and Ashley went one way and Michael and Mum went the other. After a few too many drinks for Dad at the Mexico pavilion—which, as always, had the A/C set to a temperature that would've been more appropriate at Norway next door—Dad and Ashley stumbled around the lagoon toward the UK. He wanted to see if they could find his namesake hanging about, good ol' Bert from *Mary Poppins*.

"Dick van Dyke," he reminded Ashley, as she, his seventeen-year-old daughter, helped his drunk ass stay upright.

"Yep," she said, knowing that he'd only mentioned the actor's name to set up his favorite joke.

"You know," said Dad, "that's not his real name."

"Is that right?" said Ashley, playing along.

"Nope," said Dad. They were staggering past Canada, most of the way to their destination, when he gave her the final bit of set-up. "van Dyke is his *stage* name," Dad told Ashley, drawing it out. "You're gonna be Hannah Hamilton," he said, "just like he became Dick van Dyke."

"And what was his real name, Dad?"

"Penis de Lesbian," he said, and he laughed so hard that he

stumbled over his own feet. Ashley had to deposit him on a bench to keep from throwing her back out.

"Dad," she said, once he stopped laughing. "Are you okay with this? With what I told you this morning?"

"You're really not going to go to college?" he asked.

"I'll go this year," she told him. "Because it's already paid for. But Dad," she said. "I don't want the debt. I don't want *you guys* to have the debt. It's not worth it."

"But we saved for you," he said. "There's a fund."

"Dad," she said. "The greatest gift you could give to me is to let me graduate into the world on my own terms. Think of everything I could do with my life if I didn't owe my first-born child to that old bitch Sallie Mae."

"Sallie Mae?" he said, raising an eyebrow in confusion.

"Student loans, Dad. I don't want them. And I don't want some useless piece of paper that's supposed to dictate my worth. I don't need some slip of parchment that represents—I don't even *know* what it's supposed to represent."

"I wish I'd finished my degree," he said.

"Why?" she asked him, and she honestly wanted to know. Because, the truth was that her father would've gained nothing from a degree. He was a musician and a disc jockey, and he'd learned way more in his life just by living it than he ever would have if he'd dicked around some ivy-covered campus for four years. Did he really need a bunch of capped and gowned fuckwads to decide he was worth something?

He didn't have an answer. Instead, he reminded Ashley that Mum had finished college. And med school. And that Michael was two years in and a different man because of it.

Ashley didn't know what to say. She didn't want to hurt the old man, not any more than she already had. But she knew what she wanted out of life, and four years of carefully prescribed learning —"take two of these, and we'll quiz you in the morning"—that was *not* on her bucket list. Nor was a lifetime spent paying for the privilege of being indoctrinated into a culture that she was bent on upending.

After a minute or two, Dad started to cry.

"Dad," said Ashley, squeezing his forearm.

"I don't get it," he said.

"You don't get what?"

"I didn't abuse you," he said.

"No," said Ashley, confused.

"Did someone else?" he asked. "Did someone else touch you? Cause I'll fucking kill him," he said. And it was laughable, to imagine her father beating someone up. But Ashley didn't laugh. Because, in its own twisted way, it was sweet.

"Dad," she said, finally getting where he was going with this, "I like being naked."

He laughed again. "Sure do," he said. "Or did," he added, feeling like he needed to correct himself, maybe even feeling like the implication that he'd *ever* seen her naked, even as an infant, was improper. "We've got it on tape, you as a toddler, running bare-assed around the yard."

"And you chasing after me with a diaper in your hand," she said, smiling at him.

"Do you want me to destroy that tape?" he asked, squeezing her hand and looking worried as fuck all of a sudden. "Is it inappropriate that I still—"

"Dad!" she said, with as heavy a sigh as she ever had sighed. "Stop."

"It's one thing to be naked as a little kid," he said, stating the obvious—one of his favorite pastimes. "But you've got... you know..."

"Tits," she said, and then she remembered where they were. And for once, Ashley was the one who blushed. She looked around, but there didn't seem to be any children in earshot. It was late anyway, almost time for fireworks or some sort of show or something, and the crowds were all closer to the lagoon.

"Do you know what you're doing?" he asked her. But then, before she could answer, he sighed to himself and gave her a smile. "Dumb question," he said. "You always know what you're doing."

"There's money to be made," she said.

"Oh, I know," he said. And then a thought sobered him right the hell up. He sat up straight and he looked at his daughter more seriously than he had in years. "You gotta tell me and your brother which club it is," he said. "So, neither of us accidentally, you know—"

Ashley smirked and ruffled his hair. Then she told him "No problem, old man."

9

They were supposed to move Ashley out to Amherst that day to start college, to good ol' Zoo Mass. But when she got up that morning and headed down the stairs to see when her parents wanted to leave, Ashley found her father asleep in his easy chair. The TV was on, and they were saying something about a car crash in Paris, but Ashley was more concerned about whether her parents had had a fight. They'd had more than their share in the weeks since her announcement, and her dad was still in the clothes he'd worn out to dinner the night before.

Ashley set a hand upon his shoulder and gave him the gentlest nudge she could manage. "Dad," she said, "did you sleep out here?"

As he stirred, he pointed at the TV. "Did you see?"

Ashley crouched in front of him to look him in the eye. "Dad," she said, "did you and Ma—?"

"Diana," said her father, and he shook his head as he said it. "She was only 36."

Ashley was *so* confused. Who was Diana? Someone he'd had

an affair with? And was the fact that she was 36 supposed to make things better or worse?

He must've been awake enough to notice how befuddled Ashley looked though, because he pointed at the TV again and told her to just turn around watch. "They're going to recap the whole thing in a second," he said. "Every half hour it's the same thing…"

"In case you're just waking up," said the newscaster, "here's what we know at this hour—"

⚜

ASHLEY'S PARENTS hadn't fought the night before, but they *were* fighting by the time Michael and Robin crept out of Michael's room to help pack the car.

"*That's* what this has you thinking?!" shouted Mum.

"She was 36," said Dad, "and she'd only just started to live her life."

Mum was incredulous. If she shook her head any harder, Ashley swore it was going to roll off her shoulders, sprout a pair of feet and a wind-up key, and march across the dining room floor toward Dad like a Bob-Omb ready to burst.

"What are they talking about?" Robin asked in a whisper.

"Diana," said Ashley, as if that was supposed to explain anything. As if that was supposed to explain *everything*.

Michael asked "Diana who?"

"I suppose you see things differently," said Dad to Mum.

"She made a spectacle of herself," said Mum. "And she was killed for it."

Dad rolled his eyes as he said "They weren't *trying* to kill her."

"Weren't they?" said Mum. "Look at the fucking headlines they've got now!"

"Who was trying to kill who?!" shouted Michael, frustration at being kept in the dark finally overtaking his fear of confrontation.

"Go watch the news," Ashley told him with a sneer, as if he should have thought of that already. And so, he did. He stole out from behind Robin and into the living room.

But Robin stayed put. She didn't really care who it was that died, or who had killed her. She was more interested in watching the elder Silvers yell at each other. Coming from the broken home that she did—and from the crumbling relationship she was in with Michael—Robin was way more interested in discovering that there were cracks even in the shiniest of romantic veneers. She had never seen Doctor or Mister Silver yell—not at their kids, not at each other. Nothing. No yelling at all, until now.

"Princess Di?!" Michael shouted from the living room.

Ashley scoffed. "More like Princess *Died*," she said.

Robin was going to laugh, but Ashley's parents stopped their fight for long enough to stare their daughter down for the joke. So Robin didn't laugh. She didn't make a peep.

"What I'm saying," said Dad, returning to the fray, "is that we shouldn't be keeping Ash from doing what she wants to do. Shit like this," he said, and he pointed toward the living room and the TV in there, "should remind us that life is too short to waste on dreams that aren't yours."

"Shit like this," said Mum, pointing at the living room herself now, "should remind us that, in our sick society, if you allow yourself to be made a product—which is what your daughter wants to do, in case that's not clear—if you allow yourself to become a *thing* instead of a person, you will pay the price in the end."

Ashley turned to Robin and rolled her eyes as her parents rumbled into the next round of their bout. "Can we get out of here?" she said.

Robin nodded. "Do I have time to get dressed?" she asked.

"No," said Ashley.

ASHLEY BROUGHT Robin to the shed out back, the place where Ashley's great big dog had slept in the days before her great big sleep. "It used to be a hen house," Ashley told Robin as they crept gingerly up the rickety old ramp.

"And then Hannah made it a hen house again," said Robin, smiling at the memory of the stories she'd heard.

"Sure did," said Ashley, "but only for select clientele."

Which was true. It's not like the Silvers unleashed their lady of the evening at sundown to walk the streets, wagging her tail at any mutt who'd have her. No. Dr. and Mr. Silver kept Hannah shut up tight in the shed. But dogs of a certain size could still find their way in. There was, after all, still the hole in the east wall which led the cement ruins of what had once been the chicken coop. And so happy Hannah the Harlot became the trollop of the terriers, the courtesan of countless corgis, and the *fille de joie* for the Frenchie who lived next door.

The first time Ashley had told Robin about this, they were at the kitchen table in the Gates house. Robin was cutting the crusts off her PB&J while Ashley waited politely to go to town on her own sandwich (crust and all). And when Ashley told Robin and Mrs. Gates how many different dogs she'd seen come and go from Hannah's shed over the years, when Ash told them that Hannah's suitors sometimes chased each other around the yard out back while they waited for their turn, Mrs. Gates smiled and shook her head. Then she asked Ashley if Hannah was fixed.

Ashley nodded.

"Ah," said Mrs. Gates, smiling as she sighed. "That is the way to do it, girls. All the fun and none of the consequences."

One of her two "consequences" frowned at her. But Mrs. Gates didn't notice Robin's glum look. She was too busy trying to figure out why Ashley was laughing.

"Mrs. G," she said, "you sound jealous of my dog."

Mrs. Gates gave a quick but definitive nod. "And why not?" she said.

"Don't be too jealous," Robin told her. "Hannah's huge, and the only dogs she gets to be with are *tiny*."

"Ah," said Mrs. Gates, "but have I not told you? It's not the size of the pencil that counts, but how you write with it."

Robin rolled her eyes and asked Ashley how they even managed it. Hannah was a Great Dane for Christ's sake! How did they even reach?!

Ashley looked her dead in the eye then, and did her best impression of Jeff Goldblum from *Jurassic Park*. "Life," she said, pausing dramatically after that first word to offer Robin the rakish smile that Goldblum had offered Laura Dern, "finds a way."

And now, of course, years later, life had found a way to make Ashley the successor to her dog. Because it was in the shed that she'd stashed all the raw materials she'd collected over the past two years to make herself the new Hustler of High Street. Lingerie, platform heels, and a crate full of "sexy" costumes. She'd gotten those off a Halloween Store employee during last November's clearance, gotten them off him for the low, low price of getting him off. While she wore one, of course. Sexy Kerri Strug, as Robin recalled. Because he was super into gymnastics and had watched a tape of the Olympics every day since the ladies brought home the gold that summer. Ashley told Robin he wanted to come on her gold medal, and though she doubted his aim would be that precise, she let him give it a try. And when he *did* hit the medal, Ashley giggled and told him he should try out for the archery team in the year 2000. Or skeet shooting. Or something.

Robin sat on the floor while Ashley popped a tape into the TV/VCR combo she'd dragged out there. Ash had been watching copies of *Striptease* and *Showgirls* each night for research, seeing as she couldn't get into the club to scout the competition until she turned 18. And she'd been practicing the moves out here while she watched, while her parents thought she was mourning her dead dog.

"But she's been dead for over 2 years," said Robin.

"They don't move on as fast as I do," said Ashley.

As Ashley grabbed the controller off the top of the TV and fast-forwarded through the scene of Elizabeth Berkley fucking Kyle MacLachlan in the pool like she's having a seizure, Robin wondered if Ashley's parents had asked why she needed to drag an extension cord all the way out here.

"In the winter time," said Ashley, "I needed a heater."

"But it's August now."

She shrugged. Then she pulled her finger off the button on the remote and let a scene from *Striptease* play out. "Watch this," she said.

And so they did. They sat there in silence and watched Demi Moore appear out of the darkness in a fedora and the top half of a suit. They watched her strut down a catwalk toward a pole which plunged down from the ceiling. And they watched her take her clothes off one piece at a time, each revelation of flesh the punctuation mark on a series of tightly choreographed gyrations. When she took off her tie and proceeded to floss herself with it, from cooch to caboose and back again, Robin decided it was about the least sexy thing she'd ever seen.

Robin was about to ask Ashley why they were watching it when Ash paused the film, the movie freeze-framed now on a shot of some leering asshole in glasses who'd just swooned a little and set an elbow upon his table to steady himself. Hand on his cheek now, a sigh in his eyes, the smile on his face seemed to say "Aw shucks, ain't she purty?"

"That," Ashley told Robin, pointing at the screen, "is what I *don't* want to do."

"Then why are you watching it?" Robin asked, pushing the power button on the set so she would no longer have to look upon the face of that smitten sleazeball.

Ashley raised an eyebrow, but said nothing at first. It was only when Robin didn't say anything either, not for a long, uncomfortably silent moment, that Ashley finally spoke.

"Haven't you ever listened to a bad song," asked Ashley, "just to figure out *why* it's bad?"

Robin thought of how many times she'd listened to "We Built This City" by Starship, but she wasn't sure if that counted. It's not like she ever *chose* to listen to it. It's not like she ever sought it out. But it *was* her boyfriend's favorite song of all time, for some inexplicable reason, and she *had* spent at least some time trying to figure out why the phrase "knee-deep in the hoopla" made her want to slit her wrists.

"Okay," said Robin. "I see your point." Then Robin asked if, seeing as Ashley was 18 now—"Happy birthday, by the way!"—was she finally going to start doing her research at the club instead.

Ashley nodded. "Starting tonight, if I can."

"But what about college?" asked Robin. Ashley had promised to go for the year, after all, and she wasn't one to break her word.

"They're not going to make me go," said Ashley, nodding in the direction of the house. "Not now."

Robin shook her head. Even though Ash seemed *so* certain that this was what she was going to do, Robin didn't believe she would do it in the end. Like Ashley's folks, Robin thought the one year of college would push the desire straight out of her, that some Gen Ed class in that first year, however dreadfully boring on the whole, would spark an interest in her beyond comics and video games and getting naked.

But now she wasn't going to go, and there was nothing to stop her.

"Thank god for Princess Died," said Robin, "I guess."

Ashley rolled her eyes.

"What?" said Robin, laughing uncomfortably. "You're allowed to make the joke, but I'm not?"

"Some unfunny things," said Ashley, "are only funny once."

As they handed the bouncer their IDs that night, he told the two of them that amateur night wasn't for another couple of days. Then he caught sight of Ashley's birthday and looked up at her with a smile. "You're just raring to go, huh?"

"She's got to do her research first," Robin told him.

"Well," he said, "we got some damn good tutors in here. But you look like a quick study," he said, handing them back their licenses. "If you want to be, you'll be up there in no time."

He pointed toward the stage and Robin cast her direction that way. There was a woman up there in hot pants and a camo half-tee, and she was working the pole like it was the dick she'd been searching for all her life. She even licked the damn thing once or twice.

"You too," the bouncer said to Robin. "Seeing as you already know how to work a crowd."

The two girls turned their attention back to him and he smiled. "Yeah," he said. "I recognized you. Read about you and your band in the *Globe* the other day. Lilith Fair," he said. "That's pretty big, right?"

Robin shrugged. "It was only the Village Stage. Most people didn't stop long enough to listen to more than half a song—"

"They're too hard-edged for Lilith anyway," Ashley told him, cutting Robin off. "And she's the only chick, so y'know..."

He nodded like he knew, though he probably didn't. The DJ was blasting "Closer" now, while Army Chick took her top off, so Robin felt sure the bouncer couldn't even hear what they were saying.

"I did get to meet Fiona Apple," said Robin. "So that was cool."

He nodded again.

"No, no, no," Ashley was saying now, now that she'd caught which song they were playing.

The bouncer laughed. "What?" he said. "You've never wanted to fuck someone like an animal?"

"That's the only way *to* fuck," she told him, and he laughed.

"So what's the problem?"

"The problem," Ashley told him, "is that this song is so fucking *obvious*" Ashley pointed at the stage. "That girl's *grand-daughter* is going to be stripping to this song one day."

He laughed some more.

"You want to dance to Nine Inch Nails," said Ashley, "you hit 'em with 'The Only Time' instead."

Now he stopped laughing. Now he sat up straight and looked at Ashley like he'd underestimated her. "*Fuck* yes," he said, and he held up a hand for a high-five.

Ashley gave him some skin and asked "You know it?"

"Do I know it?" He shook his head at her, but with a big-ass smile on his face. "I was on Lansdowne in 1989 when they came through Boston on their first tour. And I can't tell you how many girls in fishnet and pleather *still* get all up in my business when I request that tune at Manray. Even after they're all like 'But Trent hates that song now' and blah, blah, blah."

"Well," said Ashley, slapping him on the knee. "My first set here, whenever that might be, I am dancing to that song."

He laughed. "Can't wait," he said. "But for now, get your ass in there and have yourself a happy fucking birthday."

"Did I hear it's someone's birthday?" asked the next girl they saw. And when Ashley nodded, the girl whisked her away for a private dance to celebrate.

But Robin? She just watched from afar and sipped at her soda, getting to work on the two-drink minimum while she tried to catch a glimpse of what was going on behind the wall of ferns that marked off their poor excuse for a VIP section.

She was offered a dance of her own while Ashley was gone, but Robin declined. The only girl she wanted in her lap just then was

Ash, and she hadn't put herself up for grabs yet. So Robin would have to wait.

ROBIN SKIPPED her evening classes one night a couple of weeks later and drove up from Berklee to catch Ashley's debut. And Ash made good on her promise to the bouncer, sandwiching "The Only Time" between Aerosmith's "Pink" on one side (for the creepy old men in the room) and Bryan Adams' "The Only Thing That Looks Good On Me Is You" on the other (because she wanted to end on something stupid and upbeat).

It was a damn good set, too. The playful innuendo of "Pink" as she stripped down to bra and panties. The way she pretended to be intoxicated by their adoration at the end of that silly song, falling back against the pole and sliding to the floor while it faded out. The way she lurched forward toward the tip rail of the catwalk as the next song began, so that when Reznor proclaimed "I'm drunk" to the one-two slap of his electric bass it wasn't clear if she was going to ralph all over Ralph (or whatever the name of the nearest patron was) or if she was about to kiss him. Ashley timed it so well, the way she whipped her head back and forth to the beat, that she was looking straight into the dude's eyes when Reznor sang "and right now I'm so in love with you." Then she used the rail to balance herself and push her body toward him, like she was the little fucking mermaid singing "Part of Your World" on top of that rock, only Ashley was pushing her chest into some dude's face instead of out into the open sky.

She didn't get up off the floor at all until the chorus kicked in for the last time. Each guy who sat along the catwalk got himself a show. Whether it was something slow and methodical during the verses, during the "I don't want to think too much about what I should or shouldn't do's", something more frantic during the repetitions of "maybe I'm all messed up," or something somewhere in between, like the guy who she took her top off for. He was lost in Ashley's eyes as she reached behind her back to unclasp the bra, as she mouthed the words "Nothing quite like the feel of something new" to him while she wrapped the garment around the back of his neck to pull him closer. But when the chorus kicked in again, when she finally sprung to her feet to move her body for herself now and no longer just for him—when she did that, he fell back into his seat. And he was so bewildered that he stood to go.

Not before leaving a ten on the rail, though. Half the price of a lap dance, simply for scaring the shit out of him.

Or the jizz, thought Robin, smirking to herself.

By the time Ashley got to Bryan Adams, she was marching up and down the catwalk like she owned the place. And if they kept tipping her like they were, maybe someday she would. That's what Robin found herself thinking. Ashley didn't have the moves yet— she had no *idea* what the hell to do with the pole, and it was laughable the one time she tried to take a spin around it (laughable, and a bit scary)—but she made up for lack of experience with an overabundance of confidence. Even when she'd finally stripped herself bare, which she saved—as most of the girls there did—for the final half of the final song, she didn't seem scared. And when some dude put two twenties on the rail, one to get her attention straight away, one to reserve the lap dance he wanted after, Ashley didn't flinch. She sauntered over to him, fell to her knees and feigned touching herself—as if the sight of two Jacksons was enough to make her wet.

Which, now Robin thought of it, maybe it was. Maybe Ash did get off, at least a little bit, on them getting off. She sure made them believe it, and even Robin was falling under her best friend's spell back in the shadowy corner she'd made her perch. Where she'd gone to make sure she didn't make Ashley nervous. Which, of course, she needn't have worried about at all.

Ashley finished her set, and then Robin watched the strangest thing she'd yet seen in that place. Ashley got fully dressed, even though she was about to take Twin Jackson over there back behind the ferns and get naked again in like two seconds. Was there some rule about having to be fully clothed while you walked from place to place? Robin actually wondered that for a second. But then she thought of something she wished she hadn't. Robin thought of her boyfriend the painter, of the thesis he'd begun working on that summer—the one that would get him into grad school, the idea that would, a decade later, become his first book.

The juxtaposition of cloth and flesh.

That was what they were paying for, not just Ashley's body writhing on top of theirs—though that was, of course, the biggest part of it. What they wanted as well was to watch the clothes come off. They wanted the tease. Sure, what they ultimately wanted was her stripped bare while they remained safely ensconced within the armor of their t-shirts and jeans, their button-downs and their khakis. Sure: they wanted to witness the full power of their hard-earned cash (and, by extension, their hard-won manhood). But beneath it all they wanted what Michael said everyone wanted—*everyone*, back to the Greeks and their sculptures of women with their tits out even though they were draped in robes. What Ashley's customers wanted most, Michael would say, was to stand in awe of the power of the right fabric in the right place. The power of cloth to take a beautiful thing like the human body and to make it transcendent.

What Robin wanted was to fuck her. Like an animal, she supposed. To feel her from the inside.

But for now a lap dance would have to do.

And thanks to Twin Jackson over there, whose hand Ashley took now, whose wilting old body she pulled toward the promised land beyond the ferns—thanks to him, Robin still had to wait her turn.

But not for long, thought Robin. *And not forever.* Then she took the scrap of newsprint she was carrying in her wallet nowadays, the childhood keepsake she was certain had been a prank of her brother's. *Certain*, until she wasn't anymore. Robin held the scrap of newsprint in her hand and read it to herself once again:

She spent her final moments in the arms of Hannah Hamilton, the on-again off-again girlfriend who Gates called "the love of her life"

Then she looked up and caught a glimpse of Ashley dancing beyond the ferns—of *Hannah* dancing, really—and Robin smiled.

It's only a matter of time, she thought. *It's only a matter of time.*

❧ 10 ❧

On the night that Robin and Michael were Robin and Michael no more, Ashley drove down to Boston to console her friend.

She found Robin tucked into the corner of some vast, dark space the Berklee kids had packed to the gills for an open mike. And she looked amazing, standing there in the shadows—like the femme fatale from an issue of *Sin City*: all black and white and hard edges, except two splashes of red. There was the red of the flannel tied round her waist of course, but there was also the red of the lips wrapped round the thumb she was biting.

She put on makeup, thought Ashley. Even today, when she had every excuse to be a blubbering mess, she couldn't leave her room without her mask.

Ashley knew Robin didn't want to be there—the roll of her eyes between songs said as much—but she'd *promised*. She'd promised her roommate she'd come and see her play. And though Robin wasn't great at keeping promises on the whole—her indiscretions with a jazz drummer having been the straw that broke her boyfriend's back—she did remain faithful to friends. But

Ashley could see in the poorly concealed scowl on Robin's face what keeping this particular promise was costing her.

Ashley thought the band sounded fine—had to actively resist tapping her foot, in fact—but she knew what Robin would tell her later. "It only sounded *fine*," she'd say, "because the acoustics in the place are impeccable."

"You want to get out of here?" asked Ashley, as applause filled the room.

"Yes," said Robin. "*Please*."

THEY TOOK a stroll down Mass Ave without bothering to go upstairs to get Robin a coat. Her flannel, she insisted, would be enough. And even though she was shivering like a madwoman by the time they'd made it halfway to Huntington, Robin refused to take Ashley's jacket for her own. "The cold," she said, "is the only thing keeping me alive."

And perhaps it was that thought which brought them to the reflecting pool—that long, flat pond the Christian Scientists had dug alongside their mother church. Perhaps it was because of *that* —Robin's notions about the purifying power of freezing one's tits off—that the girls' long-awaited heart-to-heart happened on the stone lip which ran along the basin.

Or maybe, thought Ashley—just *maybe*—it had something to do with the fact that her brother once had the gall to compare the magnificent beauty of this place to the quaint charms of his college's tiny pond.

Robin sat first, and the shiver that came over her then was more like a shudder. So when Ashley took off her jacket this time, Robin didn't refuse. As Ashley draped it over her shoulders, Robin even reached up to give Ash's hand a squeeze.

And she didn't want to let go.

So Ashley stood behind Robin as they got to talking, and it

may even have been her fingers working to untie the knots in Robin's shoulders which drew the first words from that confused girl's lips.

"You're better at that than Michael," she said.

"Painters rely on a delicate touch," said Ashley, making excuses.

Robin sighed a sigh then that was really half-moan.

"Musicians, too," said Ashley, teasing.

"Some of us," said Robin, in between the gasps Ashley drew out of her as she hit spot after spot, "some of us know that there's a time to be gentle and a time to be—"

"Rough?" said Ashley, pulling at a knot that was pissing her off.

"Yes," said Robin softly. And then she sniffled.

Ashley took that as her cue, so she came round to the front and took a seat. And it was *freezing*, but she did her best to suppress the shiver because she knew what Robin was going to say.

"What are you wearing?!" she asked, pinching the fabric of Ashley's skirt between thumb and forefinger.

"It's comfy!" Ash protested with a giggle.

"For a spring afternoon maybe!"

Ashley grabbed Robin's hand and set it back on her own leg. Then she held it there.

"You do that better than Michael, too" is what Robin said as she nodded her chin at their intertwined fingers.

Ashley smiled as she rolled the knuckle of Robin's thumb between her fingers. "You only think so," she said, "because the two of you were together for so long."

"No," said Robin, "there were some things he was still pretty good at."

"Well," said Ashley, and she leaned in to feign a whisper. "I left my strap-on at the office."

Robin let her forehead fall against Ashley's then. "A shame," she told her, "but you're good with your fingers. So there's that."

Ashley brushed her lips against Robin's, not sure if this was the moment or if maybe it was the next one. So she pulled back a smidge, just enough to look Robin in the eyes, and she said "I'm pretty good with my tongue, too."

They held there for a moment, just looking at each other, before Robin tugged at Ashley's bottom lip with both of her own. She held on for just a moment, then let go. And she gave a little sigh then, that tiniest of exhales. It was such a small bit of breath —such a *small* noise—but every bit of tension within her seemed to make its escape in that moment. She'd done it. She'd kissed Ashley—or half-kissed her, at least—and Ash hadn't pulled away. And the world hadn't ended either, not in a bang nor in a whimper. And Ashley was smiling at her. Ashley didn't hate her. She maybe even liked her.

Maybe.

And, Robin realized all of a sudden, her roommate was gone for the night—off partying with her band somewhere off-campus to celebrate their first show. What kind of providence was this? On the night that everything was finally happening, Robin had her room all to herself.

"I'm hungry!" Robin announced, apropos of nothing. And when Ashley asked her if that was a euphemism, if *she* was what was on the menu, Robin said "No, not yet. I just realized I haven't eaten all day."

᭡᭢᭡

THEY SHARED a slice of pizza at a place near campus that took Robin's meal plan dollars as payment, since the only thing she had on her was her student ID and the key to her room—and since she insisted that she pay, since Ashley had driven all the way down to Boston to see her.

"It's only a forty-five minute drive," Ashley tried to say, but Robin wasn't having it.

"Besides," Robin said, "one of their slices is a meal for two anyway."

And so, she cut it in half with a plastic knife she had to beg for from the annoyed chick behind the counter. And while Robin used a napkin to soak up some of the grease, Ashley went right to town on her half of the slice.

"I don't know how you guys do that," said Robin, frowning. Then she balled up her greasy napkin inside a fresh one and set it aside.

"Listen," said Ashley, setting down her slice, "if you mention my brother again, I am *not* fucking you tonight."

Robin laughed.

"We can cuddle," said Ashley. "But that's it."

It looked like Robin was going to laugh again, but something in Ashley's demeanor must've changed her mind. Because then she looked scared for a second, like she was worried she'd ruined things.

Ashley squeezed Robin's knee to let her know that she hadn't. Then they ate in silence.

WHEN THEY GOT BACK to Robin's dorm room, the first thing Ashley noticed was the camera with the big honking lens on it. It was sitting atop the little end table where Robin usually tossed her keys, so Ashley asked "Who belongs to that?"

Robin groaned. "Her boyfriend," she said, shaking a thumb towards the top bunk. "He goes to Mass Art."

"You think they'll be back for it?" Ashley asked, closing and locking the door.

Robin looked positively deflated as she shrugged. Then she sat down on the edge of her bed and shook her head at the floor.

"You and Michael never did it while she was around?" asked Ashley.

Robin looked up at her wide-eyed. "What happens if *you* bring him up?"

"Well, let's find out," she said.

Ashley swayed her hips as she sauntered toward Robin, giving her a taste of what the customers got when they at sat alongside the club's catwalk. And when Ashley saw Robin smirk at the sight, she started to hitch up her skirt. She pulled it up inch by inch, showing Robin a bit more leg with every step she took towards her. A bit more, and then a bit more. And then a bit more. So that by the time Ashley sat astride her and let go of the cloth she'd collected in each fist, Robin's arms disappeared beneath the waves of skirt that crashed over her lap.

Robin closed her eyes and ran her hands along Ashley's legs—from knee to thigh, from thigh to hip—and she looked enthralled. She looked thoroughly entranced by the feel of Ashley's smooth skin beneath her calloused fingers. But then her thumbs drifted just a bit higher, headed toward Ashley's waist and her eyes shot open at what her thumbs found.

Or, rather, at what they *didn't* find.

"Occupational hazard," Ashley explained. "I spend so much of my time doing underwear as a performance now," she said, "that I prefer to go without whenever I can."

Robin started to pull her hands away, but Ashley grabbed at them through the skirt and pulled them back to where she was sure they were headed in the first place. Back, back, all the way back. And then down, of course, until Robin had a hand cupped around each cheek.

Robin gave Ashley a squeeze and shook her head. "Even firmer than I imagined," she said. "Like, just *how?*"

"Well," said Ashley, pulling the collar of Robin's flannel away from her neck, then pushing it down off her shoulders, "I do a *lot* of squats."

"I *hate* squats," is what Robin said as Ashley buried her face into the crook of Robin's neck.

Ashley came up for air long enough to tell her that they were worth it in the end. Then Robin had the nerve to ask Ashley how.

Ash stood and pulled Robin up with her. Then she grabbed a pillow off Robin's bed and threw it on the floor.

"What are you doing?" Robin asked, looking over her shoulder at the pillow.

But Ashley didn't answer. She grabbed Robin's chin and made the girl face her. Then Ash finished the kiss Robin had started back by the reflecting pool. And it had exactly the effect Ashley had hoped for. Robin went weak in the knees, and that made it all the easier to lay her down on the floor. And only once Robin's head was on the pillow did Ashley unlock their lips and stand over the other girl.

Ashley waited for a moment for Robin to ask again what was she was doing or what was going on, but Robin said nothing. She just looked up at Ashley and bit her lip, holding a hand to her heart in a silent plea for it to slow down just a bit. Ashley almost felt sorry for it, that helpless organ that didn't know what to do with itself now that it had finally gotten what it had longed for for so long.

She *almost* felt sorry, but she didn't.

With her eyes on Robin's for as long as they could be, Ashley took one step forward and then another. And then another. She stepped forward until Robin's face had disappeared from view, until she felt certain it was in the right place. Then Ashley did half a squat as a tease, and she heard Robin giggle beneath her, hidden away in the shadows of her skirt. But Robin didn't giggle at all when Ashley did a full squat the next time around. She didn't make a peep. And by the third time Ashley lowered the boom, so to speak, Robin decided to do something altogether different with her mouth.

Ashley found the feeling delightful, the feeling of a mouth on her that knew what it was doing. And when Robin's tongue prized her open and found the prize that it was looking for, Ashley fought to catch her breath. She almost sank to her knees right then to let Robin have her way with her, but Ashley wasn't done having her way with Robin.

Despite the angry protests of her clit to stay put, Ashley rose up out of her squat.

But beneath her, Robin clenched hands round both calves to keep Ashley from getting away entirely. Then Robin told her she was a bitch. A *tease*.

Ashley laughed as she told Robin "You have no idea." Then she worked to unwrap the skirt from around her waist. And yes, of course, she swayed her hips as she did it. A little dance, just for Robin, because Ashley was *always* putting on a show. Even when she wasn't, because she just couldn't help it.

"You are not getting away this time" is what Robin said to her as she tossed the skirt aside, as she looked down at Robin waiting for her between her splayed legs.

"Oh," said Ashley, smirking. "Is that right?" And Ashley thought to herself, *I'm going to tease her at least twice more before I give in. I can hold out that long.*

But when Ashley sank into her next squat, Robin made good on her promise. She grabbed hold of Ashley's hips so hard that Ash gave up the game right then and there. She fell to her knees, careful to give Robin enough room to breathe, and let her get back to business.

❦

WHEN THEY WOKE the next morning in Robin's bed, it was to a flash of light so bright it might have been a new world being born. But, judging by the way Robin's roommate was yelling at her photographer boyfriend, the culprit was something far more mundane.

"What the fuck?" screeched the roommate. "You can't do that, Simon. Give me that fucking camera."

"No way, man," said the boyfriend. "Do you know how much the *Herald* will pay for this? With Miss 'My Band's on the Cusp of a Record Contract' over there wrapped around her boyfriend/bandmate's naked sister? His *sister*, of all people!"

Ashley extricated herself from Robin's embrace and stood to face the motherfucker. The roommate averted her eyes when she realized Ashley wasn't wearing a damn thing except for the hickeys Robin had left on Ashley's thighs, but the boyfriend? He couldn't look away.

"Give me the camera," said Ashley, stepping toward him.

"Or what?" he said, holding it behind his back.

"Give me," said Ashley, holding out a hand, "the *camera*."

Robin could see him trembling as Ashley stared him down. She could see he had no idea what to do with her, a chick who looked like she was ready for a fight even with her tits hanging out. There was a bead of sweat rolling down his temple, then his cheek, as Ashley stood there waiting for him to hand it over. And he was about to say something, he was about to lay it on her—his rationale for being a dick—when Ashley laid him out instead. She threw a left hook into the side of his pretty little face and watched him collapse toward Robin's roommate. Who did absolutely *zilch* to break his fall, it turned out. Because she was too busy apologizing to Robin, after all.

Ashley picked the camera up off the floor and told Robin she had an idea.

"That's my..." Simon began to say, but Simon *didn't* say. He couldn't even finish his sentence before he passed out.

"What's the idea?" Robin asked, as her roommate knelt over her prone boyfriend to check if he was still breathing.

IN THE YEARS TO COME, everyone would remember the headline —"Boston's Most Notorious Rock and Roll Slut Goes Solo"—but nobody would remember that it was Ashley who came up with the nickname.

The *Phoenix* would get all the credit, but Ashley was the one who spent a week scribbling down variations on the theme while she was backstage at the club. That week between when they first showed the editor the photo and when the paper's best writer sat them down for the interview—that was a whirlwind of meetings. There was Robin and Michael and Billy sitting at the Dunk's in Drum Hill to break up Gideon's Bible for good, Robin meeting with the label to finalize the deal that it turned out they'd wanted all along (Robin, minus the boys), and the two girls meeting with Robin's roommate's now *ex*-boyfriend to hand him back his camera and a month's worth of Ashley's tips in exchange for not raising a stink.

When it was time for the interview, they arranged with the strip club's owner to hold it in a darkened corner of the place—all while girls worked the pole for the lunchtime crowd. The establishing shots the writer would paint for his readers were well worth the headaches they all had afterward from trying to hold a coherent conversation over the throb of the drums and bass.

And though the piece was all about Robin, they'd decided to position Ashley as the Yoko in the story, the new partner—the new *muse*—so she had to be there too. Which meant it was no surprise that the interviewer had a couple of questions for her. Like the one he ended with, for instance:

"And, before we wrap up," he said, "I just wanted to ask you, Ashley, how you feel about dating someone who was so notably unfaithful to your brother all these years."

Ashley laughed. "How do I feel?" she said. "About dating Boston's most notorious rock and roll slut?"

And *god*, how he got to scribbling when she turned that phrase.

"I feel great," said Ashley. "I've finally found a woman who's woman enough for me."

"And you're not worried," said the interviewer, flipping to the next page of his notepad even as he spoke, "you're not worried that she'll sleep with someone else while she's off on tour?"

"Worried?" said Ashley, and she laughed again. "That's part of our deal, man. Robin and Michael, they had *one* autumn of 'anything goes.' Well, man, I am the *Ashley* of Anything Goes."

"So..." said the interviewer, flabbergasted and fighting for a way to phrase his follow-up.

"So," Robin told him, "we do what we want—"

"And fuck who we want," Ashley added.

"And then we come home to each other," said Robin. "We are," she said, "and always will be, as good ol' Bob put it, each other's shelters from the storm."

They didn't print that part. "Cut for space," they told Ashley by phone when she called them on it. But the girls knew why it was the paper did what they did. You can feed a newsman all the talking points you want, but even the weakest willed amongst that spineless species will find themselves a point of view eventually. An angle, if you will. And two girls in love, in a kind of love without any of the boundaries that society took to be the pillars of that sacred emotional institution—no one was ready for that. So they presented Ashley and Robin as nothing but a pair of sluts, ready to take on the world.

But that was only part of the story.

.

❧ III ❧
WHEN YOU WON'T TAKE IT FROM ME

2001-2005

11

A couple years later, since everyone was cool with everyone else again, Ashley invited Robin to be her plus-one at Michael's wedding. And it was during the run-up to that blessed event that the story of Robin Gates and Ashley Silver took its next turn.

Michael and his fiancée had decided to get married at the family's house down the Cape, with Nantucket Sound and Red River Beach as their backdrop. But none of the reception halls nearby had caught their fancy, so Michael and Ashley's cousin Veronica—she who ran the house down there now—suggested digging out and finishing the root cellar and walk-out basement of the old barn. It was right there, she said, right next to where they were going to have the ceremony anyway, so why not?

And that was how they came to learn the truth about a certain witch who'd once lived on that property, a woman named Ada who'd had quite the influence on everything that had thus-far come to pass.

It was this excavation which revealed to the Silvers that, despite all they'd been told to the contrary, their great-grandfather's fourth wife wasn't buried beneath the pretty stone at the cemetery downtown. No. She'd been laid to rest in a shallow grave not a hundred feet from where their ancestor, her *husband*, had strangled her to death.

❧

"WHY ARE YOU EVEN STILL DIGGING?" That's what Ashley asked Veronica when she and Robin showed up that morning. "The wedding's in a month."

They were standing on the lawn, the beauty of the dawn's early light diminished by the flashing blues of a squad car.

"We were thinking of trying to get another bathroom in there," said Veronica.

"But you already have two," said Ashley.

"Yes," said Veronica. "But your father's going to be there, and have you ever timed one of that man's potty breaks?"

"Right," said Ashley. She was going to make some joke at her father's expense, but just then they all heard the tell-tale creak of the nosy next-door neighbor's screen door opening.

"Jesus," said Veronica, "the last thing I need right now is Decrepit Old Doris poking her nose in where it doesn't belong."

But the person who rounded the fence a moment later was not diminutive Doris Brown. Not at all. It was instead a nearly seven-foot-tall moving monument to muscles and masculinity.

"Holy shit," said Robin, squeezing Ashley's arm. "*Who* is that?"

"Oh," said Veronica, "that's just Ryan. Doris' nephew. Or great-nephew. Or something. He's just down here for the weekend checking in on her. He plays basketball, I think."

"Y'all okay over here?" asked Ryan as he joined the little group by the curb. "Auntie was concerned."

Veronica laughed. "How concerned?" she asked him. "The mesh of the screen door imprinted on her cheek yet?

"Just about," said Ryan, with a chuckle. Then he stopped

himself as he caught sight of Robin. He took a step back as his jaw dropped. "Yo!" he said, sounding positively flabbergasted. "You're Robin and the Redheads." He looked over one of her shoulders, then the other. "Where the redheads at? Y'all had a show last night on Lansdowne, right?"

"You know my stuff?" said Robin.

"What?" said Ryan, and he raised an accusatory eyebrow. "Black man can't appreciate a little rock and roll?"

"Nah," said Robin, blushing. "I just..."

"Ryan knows his shit," said Veronica, nodding. "His grandmother, Doris' sister—"

"Played on a record with Vern's gramps," said Ryan, pointing. "*Way* back in the day."

And this is where Ashley finally chimed in. "Shut up," she said. "Your grandmother was Marley Brown?"

Ryan gave Ashley a smile then that made her finally understand what the old gals meant when they talked about going weak in the knees. She was lucky Robin still had a hand on her back to keep her upright.

"Damn," Ryan said to Ashley. "You know my grammy's shit?"

"Hells yes," said Ashley. "I think I like her side of the record more than I like my grandfather's."

"Nah," said Ryan, shaking his head. "Nah. Thank you for being nice and all—"

"I'm *not* being nice—"

"She's not nice," said Robin, grinning at him, and Ashley could tell that it was *on* now. The game was officially *afoot*, and the game was this: which girl would have their way with Ryan first?

"My grammy's band was tight," said Ryan, "but your gramps and his outfit—they were next level. The Eli Five is some of the dopest shit I ever heard."

Just then, the cop who belonged to the cruiser emerged from the barn and made his way toward the huddled group.

"So," said Veronica to the officer, "what's the verdict?"

"Investigator's still in there doing an initial assessment," said the officer. But then, as he started to add the "but" in there, he took a gander at the lot of them and was taken aback by at least one of the new faces he found there. Ashley thought for a second the officer must be just another fan of Robin's, but then he made it plain who he was stunned to find amongst their company.

"Holy shit," said the officer, extending a hand toward Ryan, "I'm a big fan."

"Of me?" said Ryan, shaking the proffered hand. "You sure you ain't mistaking me for P-Squared?"

"Nah," said the officer. "Pierce is great and all, but you—"

"Me?" said Ryan, shaking his head. "Nah. They're gonna cut me."

"Who's gonna cut you?" said Robin, adopting a kinda quasi-kung fu stance. "I'll *cut* them!"

The officer gave her a look, which made Robin stand up straight real fast. Then he turned back to Ryan and told him "They can't cut you, man. Who's gonna play the 2?"

Ryan shook his head. "You think they need a straight-up 2 when they got both P-Double and Toine? I'm just an afterthought, man."

"Excuse me," said Ashley, *thoroughly* confused by what the hell it was they were talking about, "but could we get back to the matter at hand?"

The officer turned to Ash and frowned. "The matter at hand, ma'am, is that there's a Boston Celtic on your lawn, and none of you seem to—"

"A Celtic?" said Robin.

Ashley turned to Veronica with her jaw slung low. "You said he played basketball."

"I do," said Ryan.

"He does," said Veronica.

The officer's radio squawked and he stepped away to take the call out of earshot. The rest of them, meanwhile, stood there for a little bit in a kind of stunned quiet. It was Ryan who finally broke the silence, but only to be deferential.

"It's not a big deal," he said. "Me playing for the Celts. Be over soon anyway, like I said. When you're drafted the same year as the Truth, it's kinda hard to stand out."

"Who," said Robin, "is the Truth?"

Ryan laughed. "New nickname for P-Squared, I guess. Couple nights ago, after Paul scored 42 against the Lakers, reporter goes into the Lakers locker room to get a quote. And Shaq pulls this guy aside to say 'Paul Pierce is the motherfucking truth.' The Truth. So I guess that's what I gotta call him now."

"Until they cut you," said Veronica. And though Ashley slapped her on the arm for being rude, Ryan laughed.

Robin and Ashley looked at each other and exchanged a tele-pathic glance, then a nod. They were damn lucky Vern was gay, because Vern and Ryan had some kind of a connection. And there was no way either of them would've been able to beat that.

"I was telling Ryan," said Veronica, "about the frame of Ada's broken old mirror."

"Yeah," said Ryan. "She was saying that every once in a while somebody messes with the thing and magic happens."

"Well, just once," said Veronica, shaking a thumb at Robin. "It's never worked for anyone else, but Robin swears—"

"It's true!" said Robin.

"It's not," said Veronica. "You'd been the best guitarist in town for *years* before you put your hands through that mirror."

"I was 17," she said.

"Yep," said Veronica. "And my point still stands."

"So," said Ryan, "she thinks I should give it a try."

Veronica laughed. "I was joking," she said. "It's just an old superstition."

"It's not!" said Robin and Ashley together, and now it wasn't Robin that everyone was all staring at. It was Ashley.

"It worked for you too?" said Robin.

"It didn't work for *anybody*," said Veronica. "It's just a broken old mirror," she said, but she didn't sound convinced. Veronica even sounded a little bit scared. After all, a little over a year ago, somebody had slipped a magic potion into her evening tea, and the resulting mind-trip had convinced her to change everything about her life.

But she hadn't told any of the others about that yet, had thought it sounded preposterous—had spent months trying to convince herself that it *was* preposterous.

"Ashley?" said Robin. "Did it work for you, too?"

"Yeah," said Ryan, "inquiring minds wanna know."

Ashley shook her head. It had never worked for her—or *on* her, as she put it. But it had worked on someone else, someone she loved.

❧

"In 1950," said Ashley, "the Victorian that our great-grandfather built for Ada, which had stood abandoned for the six years since that old bastard's death—in 1950, that monstrosity of a house finally burned to the ground. Everything on our family's land turned to ash. Or, well, *almost* everything. The barn, it turned out, stood entirely untouched.

"It was a strange sight, according to the neighbors. The fire just seemed to stop when it got within a few feet of the barn. It should've kept going. There was plenty left to burn. But the neighbors, when they called my Grampy to let him know what had happened, the said it was like the eye of God was on that place, and not even the flames of hell were going to touch it.

"Most of the heirlooms were inside the barn, where Grampy and Grammy had moved them during their odd trips to check in on the place during the summers. Among these, seated in places of honor atop a table built from the scraps of some old boat, were the few trinkets that Gramp actually cared about: a mangy old boot that was said to belong to an ancestor who'd drowned at sea, the collection of Shakespeare that seemed to give Gramp's father the only pleasure in his life, and a dress that had belonged to Gramp's mother. But outside the barn, buried beneath the hills of ash where the house once stood, there was one final relic that my grandparents would hang onto: an ornate mirror that had once belonged to Ada—the wife Gramp's father had built the house for.

"'It's beautiful,' said Grammy when she found it. But then, reading the inscription on the back, she asked her husband a question she should never have asked. 'Who was Ada?' said Grammy.

"Somewhere inside the darkest corner of that mirror," said Ashley, and she looked like she was going to cry now, "somewhere in that mirror, the spirit of old Ada seethed. She would not be so easily forgotten."

"WHEN GRAMPY BUILT a new house on the land a few years later —the modest cottage that would be passed down through the family from then on—they hung his mother's dress in the closet, they placed the boot and the books upon the shelves, but they also brought the mirror into the house. Grammy couldn't bear to part with it.

"Ada wouldn't let her.

"Years later, she and I would play dress-up in front of it. That was our spot. Up there in the play room, a chest of old clothes open at our feet, we'd pretend to be anything and everything: princesses and priestesses, prophets and pop singers. My favorite was when I was Little Red Riding Hood and my grandmother pretended to be the wolf who was pretending to be a grandmother. I was little, so little that I shouldn't remember any of this, but I do. And not just because of the stories others have told me over the years. I *remember*.

"The first time we caught Grammy talking to the mirror, Veronica was six and I was two. Vern was carrying me on her bony hip, trying to prove she was a big girl. Trying, and struggling. We came up the stairs into the play room and found Grammy standing there in front of the mirror, talking to it the way she talked to my other grandmother when she came to visit—like they were the best of friends. Only: how could you be friends with a mirror?

"'Grammy,' said Veronica, 'who are you talking to?'

"'Right this minute?' she said, turning to us and smiling. 'A witch,' she said. And then, when she saw Veronica flinch at the word, and heard me begin to whimper, she said, 'Oh, but she's the good kind.' Then she smiled and nodded. 'Like Glinda. You remember *The Wizard of Oz*, don't you?'

"Veronica nodded. In both her house and mine, we watched it every year when it came on TV. That February or March airing of the film, that 'special presentation'—the anticipation for it started the previous October, when our fathers used a line from the film as their go-to scare tactic on Halloween. We'd be walking down our long driveways in the dark, after a long evening of trick-or-treating. We'd be salivating at the thought of the candy to come, ready to dig into our hauls, and our fathers would chant 'Lions and tigers and bears, oh my. Lions and tigers and bears.'

"So, did we remember *The Wizard of Oz*? Yes, we did.

"But the witch our grandmother was talking to—she was no Glinda. She might once have been, but no longer. She was more like Elphaba, the witch everyone forgot the name of and just called Wicked instead.

"Grammy was talking to Ada.

"When Veronica handed me back to my mother later, so that

I could take a nap, she told Mum about what we'd seen. But Mum just patted her head and begged her not to worry. 'It's just part of Grammy getting older,' she said.

"Veronica asked if she was sure.

"'I'm a doctor, sweetheart.' That's what Mum said. She was a doctor, and she was sure."

"THE DAY GRAMMY DIED, I tried to break the mirror so I wouldn't have to look at it anymore. I threw my alphabet blocks at it, one by one until I saw that they weren't making a scratch. Then I threw two at a time. Then three.

"With our parents making arrangements downstairs and leaving us to our own devices up in the play room, it wasn't long before all of the cousins got in on the act. Veronica smashed her ukulele against the mirror, because she'd seen something like that in a movie our dads had rented that summer for the new-fangled VCR they'd splurged on. Michael picked up his Millennium Falcon, proclaimed that Han Solo had just been shot out of the sky by Darth Vader, and flew that honking hunk of plastic right into the glass. Matt, who was the oldest, picked up the wooden rocking horse that none of us had ever seen leave the floor, and he ran at the mirror like he ran at the catchers in little league who tried to keep him from home plate. But the mirror didn't budge. It was Matt and the rocking horse that fell to the floor.

"We looked at him for some clue about what to do next. He was the closest to a grown-up in the room, so we'd follow his lead. If he cried, then we'd cry. If he decided to give it another go, then so would we. But he didn't cry, and he didn't get up to take another shot. Nope. He just laid there with the rocking horse across his chest and laughed.

"So we laughed, too.

"When the parents came upstairs to check on us, they found us huddled around the old looking glass with a box of crayons, each of us taking turns drawing on it. Veronica's dad started to admonish us for ruining a precious heirloom, but Grampy clapped a hand on his son's shoulder and said 'That blasted thing survived the flames of hell, Bobby. There ain't a Crayola in all creation that'll put a mark on it.'

"'What about burnt sienna?' asked my father. And then, as he so often did, he started laughing at his own joke.

"They all looked at him, incredulous. And because they all looked, so did we.

"He calmed his cackle to a chortle, his chortle to a chuckle. Then he repeated himself. '*Burnt* sienna,' he said, emphasizing the first word. 'Get it?'

"It was one of his greatest clunkers of all time, but they laughed at it like he was fucking George Carlin. And so did we."

"IT SPENT a lot of years under a sheet, that mirror. When Matt first read *The Lord of the Rings*, he held up the heavy tome, as substantial-looking as the Bible and then some, and he convinced us that the mirror was a direct line to the most evil creature in the universe. Matt told us that we had better stay away from that mirror if we didn't want to get got by Sauron.

"None of us had read Tolkien, but I had an X-Men comic where the villain was this talking pterodactyl-man who shared a name with Tolkien's big bad. And when I pulled it out of the short box I hauled with me to the Cape House each summer, the rest of the cousins agreed that dude looked frightening as fuck. Even Matt—who never bothered to say that, well, actually, that's not the Sauron you're looking for."

"On my tenth birthday, after a huge fight with my mom about my vanity and what it would cost me, I ran the playroom. To the mirror.

"I yanked the sheet off and stared at it for the first time in nearly seven years. But Ada didn't show herself to me. That wasn't part of her plan. She'd driven one of us nuts, and she felt confident—at that point, at least—that *that* would be enough. So she left me alone. She left *all of us* alone after what she did to Grammy, whatever it is she did. She didn't need to destroy the rest of us. She knew that soon enough, in our grief, we'd destroy ourselves.

"And it started right that very moment.

"I looked at the mirror and I couldn't stand it anymore. But this time I didn't reach for something else to help me break it. This time I decided to break that mirror with my bare fucking hands.

"I balled up a fist, wound up, and threw a haymaker at that thing.

"And that's when it broke. That's when it shattered into a million pieces that—and I swear this is true—turned to dust even as they were falling to the floor.

"I looked at my hand, expecting to see blood, and found none. There wasn't a scratch on me.

"Downstairs, my mother called me to dinner. We had to get started now, she said, because we still had cake and ice cream to do, then presents, then the annual board game to round out the summer.

I threw the sheet back over the mirror, then I ran downstairs to reap the spoils of my tenth year on earth."

As she wrapped up the story, Ashley shook her chin in the direction of the cop. He was finally coming back.

"They just found another one," he said.

Veronica ducked her head and started to shake it.

"Another what?" asked Ashley.

The officer clenched up his jaw a little bit and did his best to keep his gaze steady. "Another body, ma'am." That's what he said. "We believe the structure, your family's barn, may have been built atop an old—and probably, just to put your mind at ease and to be fair to your ancestors, *unmarked*—burial ground."

"We're living in a Stephen King novel," said Veronica, still shaking her head.

"Well," said Robin, "let's just hope it doesn't get Lovecraftian."

❧

BECAUSE THE COP wanted them all to stay close to make statements after he was done with Veronica, Robin and Ashley took Ryan back up the hill and onto the main floor of the barn. That's where, Veronica told them, she'd moved the mirror's empty frame. Her young daughter, Tracy, had apparently found it too creepy to keep up in the main house.

The coverlet which had hidden the truth of the ghastly thing for so long—that was gone. The frame stood empty, next to the shelf of Ada's things. Robin wanted to ask Ashley so many things about the story she'd just told—but then Ryan was standing beside the mirror, and the top of it barely came up to his chest, and they were all laughing so hard that it hardly seemed the time to broach such a serious subject.

"You want me to step through that?" asked Ryan.

"What's the matter?" Ashley joked. "Contortion isn't among your many talents."

Ryan pointed at Robin. "She just put her hands through, though."

"I play guitar," said Robin. "My hands were the only tool in need of an upgrade.

"Don't you talk to the man about upgrading his tool," said Ashley. "He might get self-conscious."

Robin smacked her as Ryan laughed.

"And we haven't even seen it yet," said Ashley. "It might be the most capable tool in the world," she said.

Ryan shook his head at them. "What if I get stuck?"

"She's tight," said Robin, "but she isn't *that* tight."

Now Ashley smacked her.

"I meant" he said with a chuckle, "what if I get stuck inside the mirror?"

"We'll figure something out," said Ashley.

Gingerly, Ryan stepped toward the frame. Then he turned and stepped through it sideways with one leg. "Fuck," he said, "you weren't kidding about it being cold."

"What?" said Ashley. "You actually feel something?"

"Shit yeah," said Ryan, as he ducked and bent to get the upper half of his body through. "Ouch."

"It wears off," said Robin. "I swear."

But if it did wear off, it didn't wear off for a while, because once Ryan had gotten his second leg through and was one-hundred percent out the other side, he was shivering like nobody's business.

Ashley looked around for a coat, a blanket—something—but came up empty. By the time she turned around, Robin already had herself wrapped around one half of him. But this wasn't a competition anymore. She was just trying to keep him warm. She nodded at Ashley to come round to his other side and do the same.

"What'd I just do?" he asked. Then he turned his head ever so slightly toward Robin. "Am I gonna be alright?"

"Better than alright," she said. "Just give it time."

IN THE YEARS TO COME, Ashley would wonder often: what if? What if Ryan *hadn't* stepped through the mirror that day. Would his team have had the same miraculous comeback in the back half of the season? Would they have even made it to the finals, let alone won the championship? Would they have continued to win in such new and fantastic ways, year after year?

But she could never be sure, would never *feel* sure about anything regarding that mirror, or Ada, or any of it. All she did know was that Ryan was one of two people that mirror ever had any effect on—after she broke the glass, that is.

And it would be years before they figured out why.

༺❀༻

THE POLICE LET the wedding continue as planned, with the caveat that the location of the proposed new bathroom be sealed off until after the festivities, when the investigation would resume. But the first news about the remains they found came in pretty quickly.

"One of them," Veronica told Ashley, as the two of them were zipping each other into their bridesmaids' dresses, "one of the bodies was *not* an ancient burial."

"For serious?" Ashley asked her.

She nodded. "They think she died in the late 1800s."

"She?" said Ashley. "You think it could've been one of the wives? One of our great-grandfather's seven wives?"

Veronica shrugged. "It already feels like we're in an episode of *The Twilight Zone*," she said. "So why not?"

But then Ashley screwed up her face and raised an eyebrow. Because weren't all the wives buried in the cemetery next to the congregational church?

"Who knows?" said Veronica. "You know what Matt thinks, given all the time he's spent with his nose buried in the old witch's journal."

"Ada," said Ashley. "You really think Old Silas killed her?"

There was a knock on the door. A loud one.

"What I think," said Veronica, "is that the bride's going to kill *us* if we don't finish getting ready."

12

When Ashley and Robin broke up for the first time, it was because Robin wouldn't show Ashley the note. When they broke up the second time, it was because Robin caught Ashley ransacking her apartment in search of the thing. When they broke up for the third time, it was because Robin finally told Ashley what it said.

That's when Ashley decided she was going to change the future. Right there in the penthouse of the Hotel Monteleone, a block from the Bourbon Street bars where she'd been dancing all weekend.

"What if I die anyway?" said Robin. She slapped the lid of Ashley's suitcase shut and sat down upon it. "Hmm?" said Robin, waiting for an answer. "Do you really want me to die alone?"

Ashley squatted, lifted Robin out of the way, then deposited her onto the bed. Then she got back to packing. It didn't take her long, though. She liked to travel light, that girl. Unencumbered.

Robin sprung from the bed and rushed to the balcony. She threw open the curtains, yanked open the door, and stepped out into the rain.

"What are you doing?" said Ashley. "You're going to ruin your makeup," she said. "And you're playing the fucking Superdome in two hours."

"You want me to die alone," said Robin, leaning out over the balcony's railing, wondering what would happen if she tried to end things early. If she tried to end things right fucking now. "I can't believe it," she said. "The love of my life wants me to die alone."

"I don't want you to die at all," said Ashley, zipping up her suitcase.

Robin stood on the balcony, looking out over the French Quarter, and thought about the man for whom this suite was named—"the man for whom the bell tolls," she mumbled to herself. She thought about how he'd ended it all, with the shotgun he'd used so often it might have been a friend—that's how the quote went, wasn't it? Robin thought about the inevitability of it all, of everything. Then she spoke aloud once more.

"You may not want me to die," she said, "but it's going to happen, Ashley. Everything else already has."

Robin heard the door creak open behind her. She turned and rushed back into the room.

"Ashley!" she shouted.

Holding the door open with her foot, her duffel in one hand and her suitcase in the other, Ashley looked over her shoulder to say "There is no fate but what we make."

Robin, catching the reference, scoffed. "If you're going to quote *The Terminator*," she said, "there's another line I'd much rather you say right now."

They stared at each other in silence for a moment, then two, but Ashley still wouldn't say it. So Robin did her best Arnold impression and said it for her.

"I'll be back," she said.

Ashley smiled, but she didn't say another word. And then she was gone.

AFTER THE SHOW THAT NIGHT, after telling the band she'd catch up with them in Texas, Robin hurried off to the Gold Club. There was this blonde chick working there—cute as a button, with a thing for fishnet—and they'd been eyeing each other the night before. Robin had stopped by to watch Ashley's set, but hadn't spent one minute watching the main stage. Ashley had noticed too, had offered to introduce them, but Robin was trying to be "good"—whatever that meant, and though Ash had said "Let me know if you change your mind" before getting back to work, Robin hadn't taken her up on it. But now? Now was a different story. Robin was hell-bent on getting herself a dance—or more than that, if that price was right and the opportunity presented itself. And why not? She was a free woman again, wasn't she? And she might be for the rest of her life. Maybe Ashley was only going to show up again only at the last minute, on the day Robin was going to get shot. Maybe that's how this was all going to go down, how it was all going to end. In tragedy. And if that was the case, why wait for oblivion to swallow her whole? Why not jump into that son of a bitch's open maw right now and have a look around?

"What happened to your girlfriend?" asked the girl, as she led Robin upstairs to the private rooms.

"Left me," said Robin, downing the rest of her first drink in one swallow. "Happens a lot," she said, starting in on the second.

The girl smiled. "Her loss," she said. "Right?"

"Right," said Robin, nodding. Then she nodded at the door to the private room. "There something to drink in there?" she asked.

"There can be," said the girl, and she smiled.

"Good," said Robin. "Let's make that happen."

❧

STUMBLING out of the club as the sun came up, Robin found herself looking across the street at very familiar building. But it wasn't the oyster bar she'd seen on the way in. No. This was a building she hadn't seen in thirteen years. And the last time she'd seen it, it was in Massachusetts and not Louisiana. But there was no mistaking it: a furniture store on top that specialized in chairs, and which never seemed to be open, and a bar down the bottom. And there at the door to the bar, looking like she hadn't aged a day, was the waitress.

Ada.

"We're supposed to be closed now," she said with a smile. "But for you? I think we can make an exception."

13

Robin took a seat at the bar and Ada stepped behind it. And that's how Robin's first question ended up being "What happened to the barkeep?" instead of the myriad of other, more important queries she had on her mind.

"I'm in charge now" is what Ada said as she set a glass of water down in front of Robin.

"He left you in charge?"

"Wasn't his choice," said Ada. Then she retrieved a bottle of ibuprofen from beneath the counter and shook a pair of pills out into her open hand. She offered them to Robin.

"I thought you were a witch," said Robin as she grabbed the pills.

"This stuff," said Ada, screwing the cap back onto the bottle, "is way more effective than anything I ever cooked up. Cheaper, too."

"Yeah," said Robin. "The price for the flesh of a stillborn these days is just *yikes*. Inflation, am I right?"

Ada stood silent as Robin swallowed the pills, as she chased them with a long drink of water.

"So you are her?" said Robin. "You're the same one."

"The same one your girlfriend's great-grandfather murdered? Yes," said Ada. "That's me."

"Ex," said Robin. "*Ex*-girlfriend. We broke up."

"For now," said Ada, and she looked disgusted as she said it. So disgusted, in fact, that she could no longer even look at Robin. So she took off for the other end of the bar to collect a stray glass she hadn't yet cleaned up.

Robin waited until she came back to speak again. "Back in the day," said Robin, "you didn't seem so disgusted with the way my life was going to turn out. Except for the getting murdered thing, of course."

Ada slapped a wooden bowl onto the counter, then filled it with pretzels from a bag she kept behind the bar.

"What changed?" said Robin.

"The article didn't say you were going to end up with a Silver."

"Ah," said Robin through a mouthful of pretzels. Then, after she swallowed, she said "So that means you can't see everything."

"I can't see *anything*," said Ada, "except what comes into this bar."

"You're trapped?"

"For now," said Ada.

"Oh," said Robin. "A hint of optimism. That's refreshing. So," she said, "you have a plan to get out."

"Yes," said Ada. "One of my descendants will set me free."

"One of your descendants?" said Robin. "But you died before you could—"

"Not quite," said Ada. "Let me tell you a story."

"It was 1892. Silas and I had been married for two years, and his patience with me was drawing thin.

"Once I'd scraped seven flakes from the sole of the boot, I set it back inside its box and set to wrapping my gift in the plain brown paper that Silas favored for parcels and presents both. I finished off the offering with a bow strung from simplest twine, set the package upon the table, and then leaned back with a sense of satisfaction into the ornate pillows with which I'd adorned my husband's modest divan.

"I closed my eyes and breathed deep, taking heed of each inhale and exhale. Just as my mother had done, and her mother before her, and every mother back to the mother of us all. Thought was gone from me for a good long while before I found myself wondering if fortune would smile this night upon my well-laid plans. I sighed at the uncertainty, then leaned forward to take my tea cup from the table.

"I sprinkled the flakes I had gathered from the boot into the concoction I had brewed with care for a fortnight. Then I stirred with a spoon stolen from my husband's finest set. Seven times to the left, seven to the right. Satisfied, I set the spoon down upon the saucer and began to sip.

"When there was nothing left to drink, I turned the cup in my hand. And as I turned it, I spoke the incantation. 'Oh dregs,' I said, 'I plead with all my might, please bring me what I need this night.'

"Wind ruffled the curtains of the home Silas had built for me at the edge of the deep green sea, the home he'd built upon the spot where his forefathers had been building homes for the loves of their lives since time immemorial. I knew that Silas grew tired of the effort to make proud those dear departed souls who had begot him by finally begetting himself, but I would not give up. I knew that a parent's wishes—a mother's in particular—were a powerful magic. And so, as the chill of the wind made gooseflesh of my bare arms, I begged for guidance. 'Cup,' I said, 'what say you?'

"But the cup said nothing.

"Panic stricken, I yanked my necklace from its hiding place within my bodice and began to twirl it over the cup. 'Leaves of magic,' I chanted, 'leaves of must. Do not break our sacred trust.'

"Then I placed my hands gently upon my belly.

"'Oh, womb,' I whispered, "you home without a tenant—your walls will be filled this night, I promise you. Your chamber will be occupied at last!'

"On the porch, quite suddenly, there were footsteps. With all due haste, I tidied my cup and saucer. Then I crossed quickly to the door, arriving just before it opened, and presented my cheek for Silas' kiss.

"With his nose buried in some great tome as he crossed the threshold, he paid me no mind. But he must have noticed me there, for he made no move to close the door behind him. So I closed it myself and waited for him to finish.

"I was standing there for at least few minutes more before he marked his page, slapped the book shut, and turned to face me.

"'Did you know,' he said, shaking the book in my general direction, 'that Booth was an actor, dear? He played quite a bit of Shakespeare.'

"'I'm sorry,' I said, confused, smiling the demure smile I knew that Silas favored. 'Who are you talking about?'

"'John Wilkes Booth,' said Silas, replacing the book on the shelf amongst its fellows. 'The man who killed Lincoln.'

"'I'm sorry?' I said, still smiling.

"Silas raised an incredulous eyebrow. 'Abraham Lincoln,' he said. 'The President of the United States'

"'I thought,' I said with a titter, 'I thought that the president's name was Harrison.'

"With the heaviest sigh he ever did heave, Silas explained to me that Lincoln was the president when I was born and that he died several weeks later. I argued, again with that titter that I knew both annoyed and aroused him, that I should not be faulted for my failure to remember something which had happened when I was yet a mere babe.

"'Aye,' he said, 'but you can be faulted for never learning it in all the years since. My God,' he said, pushing his thinning hair back from his brow, 'I knew you were born into the mud sill of society, but I had no idea how little—'

It was then that I set two fingers to his lips to shush him. 'Husband,' I said. 'I have news for you.'

"'What news?' he said, setting his hands upon my abdomen. 'Is it the child?'

"I peered deep into his eyes, searching there for the answer the dregs dared not give me, and then pulled away. I didn't know what to do. I should have told him weeks ago that the child was gone, that there might never have been a child in the first place— that the blood, more likely than not, had just come later than usual. A trick of the moon, that prankster. I didn't know what to do, so I stalled.

"'Silas,' I said, wrinkling my nose. 'Silas, you reek. What have you been up to?'

"Silas wrinkled his own nose, confused. 'I reek?' he said.

"'You do.'

"'I can't smell a thing.'

"I seized the opportunity to steer him further away from the subject of the child, to give myself some time to plan my next move. 'Perhaps,' I said, 'you're coming down with a touch of something. For I smell it clear as—'

"'I am not sick,' he protested. 'And I do not reek!'

"Now I raised an eyebrow, albeit a less incredulous specimen than his.

"Silas raised one arm and sniffed, then the other. Then he harrumphed. 'I did,' he admitted, 'chance upon a gander pull on the way home.' Now he nodded, removing his jacket. 'That must be it. The stench of the ruffians must have clung to my coat.'

"I asked him what a gander pull was.

"'You've never seen one?' he said.

"I shook my head no.

"'Perhaps you were born further from the mud sill than I suspected.' He smiled and shook his head. Silas loved the chance to explain things. As chance would have it, I *had* laid eyes upon the spectacle in question more than once in my youth. But Silas didn't need to know that, at least not at that moment.

"'They hang a goose,' Silas told me, 'upside down by its feet. Then they take turns riding by on horseback, trying to twist its head off.'

"It was quite a sight, I remembered. My father, in fact, had been quite efficient at the avocation. Too good, I recalled. The other scoundrels in his circle always held him back until the end, so as not the spoil the sport.

"'That sounds disgusting,' I said, holding back a smile at the memory of my father on horseback. Ever dashing. Even in death.

"In my moment of reverie, Silas caught sight of the box at last. 'What's in the box?' he asked. 'Ada, what is in that box?'

"'Oh,' I said. 'That.'

"'Is that your news?' he asked, his dander up, his chest beginning to heave. 'Do not continue to pile on the agony, woman. Is our child in that box? Is that your news? Have I lost another—'

"The truth spilled from me then, as if he'd cut it out of me with the sharpness of his words.

"'How long have you known?' he asked, stalking away from me, seething.

"'I know I should have told you sooner,' I said, 'but I didn't know how.'

"'I should, by now,' he said, 'no longer be astounded by the the breadth and depth of things you don't know. Alas—'

"'But I have taken steps,' I told him, a little more desperation in my voice than I would have liked. 'I know you don't always approve of my ways, but this will work. I know it. The leaves have told me so,' I fibbed. I knew they would have told me eventually, so I didn't think this an outright lie. Just a fib. A little one.

"Silas turned to face me, his face flush, his skin redder and hotter than tarnation itself.

"'The leaves?!' he shouted. 'You entrust my legacy to leaves? I tore down my mother's house for you, you ungrateful strumpet. You said it was beset by evil spirits, and I built this sprawling, garish mess in its place—*for you*. When you said the spirits might linger here still, I bedded you in every one of these eleven rooms, searching for the purest of the lot. And now,' he said, 'now you tell me that *leaves* will help us to conceive a child?'

"I breathed in deep and out slow. In deep and out slow. Then I nodded. 'The leaves,' I said, 'and the contents of this box.'

"'What is inside this box,' he asked, 'that will assure our success?'

"I smiled. 'Open, it, husband, and see for yourself.'

"I watched, with fingertips clenched between my teeth, as Silas unwrapped my gift. As anxious as he might have been to see what was inside, he still untied the knot in the twine rather than snapping my neatly built bow in half. And he still untucked one corner of the wrapping at a time, instead of ripping the paper unceremoniously from the box. But then the moment of truth came and he could not hold himself back any longer. When at last the lid of the box presented itself to him, he threw it back and stared inside.

"His face went white as he withdrew the weathered boot from its box and held it before him.

"I reached into the box and plucked from its depths the scrap of yellowed newsprint I'd hoped he would find to help explain things. But he had no eye to spare to examine the paper; both were trained on the boot.

"I read the clipping aloud to him. 'Lost overboard,' I began, 'November 13th, from the schooner Minna of Harwich, Mr. Silas Silver, aged 28 years. He has left a wife, three daughters, and a son. The man's foot, boot, and stocking, the latter marked SS (which drifted ashore early in December near P'town) belonged to Mr. S. His wife identified the mark on the stocking.'

"'Alas,' Silas mumbled, still examining the boot, 'poor Yorick.'

"'Who?' I asked.

"'I knew him well,' said Silas, a single tear rolling down his still blanched cheek. 'If only,' he mumbled. 'If only.'

"'I thought your father's name was Silas,' I said, holding the scrap of newspaper out for him to see. 'That's what it says here in the clipping. That's what you've always told me. Who's Yorick?'

"'Where did you find this?' asked Silas, finally looking at me again. He offered up the boot by way of explanation.

"I told him how I'd found it beneath the floorboards of the kitchen, how it had called out to me. I asked, 'Have you never seen it before?'

"'I haven't,' he said. 'I never saw it.'

"'You knew nothing of this relic?' I said. 'Nothing at all?'

"'Oh, yes,' he said. 'I knew. My sisters told me of it. Many nights in my youth, in those years after I was deemed old enough to know how my father died, I could think of little else.'

"Silas rose and began to pace around the edges of the room, circling me. As he continued to speak, he kept a firm grip on the boot with one hand and stroked the books he passed with the other.

"'I still remember the nightmare,' he said, 'how it haunted me. And most troubling was that it never ended the same way twice. Oh, if only there had been some sense of continuity, some sticky end I could have anticipated with dread each time, then it might have been easier to bear. But no. One night, it was the simple pain of seawater flooding my lungs; the next I might be swallowed whole by a great white whale; and the night after that I would walk the plank and plunge into the embrace of the shark below, feel my flesh torn asunder, watch my foot and my boot float off toward the shore, borne along on waves dyed red by my blood.'

"'Your blood yes,' I said. 'But your foot? Your boot?' I pointed. 'That was your father's.'

"'Oh, of course,' he said. 'But it was a curse from my father—sire many children, as he had, or suffer the same death he was suffering then.'

"'Ah,' I said, standing as he passed and taking hold of his arm to hold him steady. 'But what if he never meant for it to be a curse?'

"Silas shook me off and continued to brood. 'It's all nonsense anyway,' he said. 'We speak of his legacy as if he were prepared to bequeath it. But he had no idea. His death was an accident. He thought he'd have years to pass on what he meant to pass on.'

"I scoffed and told him that was hopelessly naïve.

"'Naïve?' he said. 'How so? Explain that to me.'

"'He was a mariner, Silas. Certainly he knew the risks of his profession.'

"'Maybe he did, maybe he didn't,' said Silas, ceasing his pacing at last. 'But that is immaterial,' he said as he collapsed into his chair. 'What matters now is why you have brought this boot before me, why you have dug up old bones best left buried.'

"I knelt before him and set my hands upon his knees, rubbing as I told him that to leave things buried was to deny their power. When he asked me 'what power?' I told him: 'The power to conceive a child.'

"Silas laughed, as great a guffaw as I had ever heard from him. 'Am I to bend you over my knee and fuck you with his boot? Am I to believe that his virility is so unmatched that my father might impregnate you from beyond that grave? That his seed might spring forth from the desiccated flesh of his big toe?'

"I tore the boot from his grasp and shook it in his face. 'Four children he sired. Four! The path he laid out for you is clear, but it is ground on which you fear to tread.'

"'What path, woman? You speak in riddles. You speak nonsense.'

"Ada shook her head. 'You're afraid.'

"Silas wrestled the boot back from me and smacked me across the face with it. And then, as I fell sideways to the floor, he rose to his full height above me. He seethed as he unbuckled his belt. 'You think it is fear that has kept me from spreading my seed? Fear?!'

"There came then a deafening crash of thunder. Both of us looked around, confused, but I soon focused my gaze on the boot.

"'The skies were clear,' said Silas. 'What mischief is this? Ada, what are you up to?'

"I smiled as the weather provided the answer that the tea leaves had not. Silas grabbed at my necklace and pulled me toward him.

"'Don't be angry,' I said. 'My love, I have done this for for the both of us. Don't you feel it?' I felt my body readying itself, hoped that his would follow suit. 'It's been a long time.'

"'Feel what?'

"'I have conjured him, Silas. I have summoned the one who can help you, who can help *us*.'

"Silas straddled me, my necklace still tight in his clenched fist. 'Conjured?' he said. 'Summoned? I don't need any help!'

"He yanked me to my feet by the necklace then, spun me around, and bent me over the arm of his chair. It wasn't the way I had imagined it, but if this was the way the spirit was to take him—if this was the way he was meant to take me—then so be it. It would all be worth it in the end. I knew this to be true. The line of his father would continue. And the line of my mother, as well. We were, each of us, the last hope of our ancestors. However he took me, whatever it cost, it was a price I was willing to pay.

"Thunder cracked again, shaking the very floorboards beneath our feet. And then, with a flash of lightning, all light was gone from the room. Rain began to pound down on the roof above and Silas seemed to have quit his business behind me. I could feel him stiff against me through the fabric of my bloomers, but my bloomers had yet to be torn asunder.

"'Silas?' I said.

"His hands squeezed my hips as he said, 'Quiet, woman! Do you hear that?'

"The front door creaked open, seemingly of its own accord. The roar of the maelstrom grew louder and louder. But through it all, if I listened hard enough, I could hear the squelching of footsteps making their way through the mud outside.

"Silas let me go and pulled up his pants. I collected myself and straightened my skirts. But neither of us made for the door. Neither of us made to close it. It was if we both knew, and had silently agreed, that there was no point to deny what was coming for us now.

"Presently, the feet we'd heard found the wood of the front steps. And then a figure began to ascend toward us, making its way toward the threshold.

"It was ghastly, this apparition. Its hat was in tatters, its top coat riddled with holes, and every inch of its body was draped in sea weed. Even the rusted musket it was using as crutch. I looked down the length of the figure and saw that, sure enough, one foot was missing.

"'Who are you?' Silas said, bellowing to be heard as he drew me to him.

"The figure made its way toward the discarded boot and plunged the stump of its severed leg into the boot's open maw. It tested the leg once, then twice, and when it was satisfied the mangled thing could take its weight, the figure cast aside its crutch, letting it thump to the floor.

"'Who are you?' Silas screamed once more.

"'Get off of her,' said the figure, its voice raspy from disuse.

"'Who are you?' said Silas.

"'I said get off.'

"The figure waved a hand at Silas, and I watched in surprise as the gesture sent my husband hurtling away from me.

"'Silas,' I asked the figure, 'is that you?'

"'What are you on about?' asked my husband as he stood and brushed himself off. 'I'm Silas.'

"I pointed toward the figure and smiled at my husband. 'Yes,' I said, 'And so is he.'

"The ghost of my husband's father began to unbuckle his belt, and I saw clearly now what was meant to be. *Whatever the cost*, I reminded myself as I bent at the waist to remove my underpants. Then I hiked up my skirts and sat myself upon the windowsill to wait.

"'No,' said my husband as the ghost made its way toward me. 'No!' he said. 'I can do this myself.'

"Husband grabbed ghost by the shoulder then, but ghost was having none of it. With a flick of his wrist, the ghost slapped his son to the floor. Then he stepped on the fallen man with his mangled leg and pulled his bloodied foot from its boot, the ruined thing clinging to the rest of him by only the thinnest threads of muscle and sinew. The boot sat atop my husband's chest as ghost turned back to me to finish his job. And my husband lay supine on the floor, wrestling with the seemingly immovable horror that pinned him to the spot.

"'Ada,' shouted my husband. 'Don't! I can do this.'

"'No, you can't!' said the ghost as he stepped out of his water-logged pants, as he set himself between my thighs. 'I never taught you, son. I didn't live long enough to show you how.'

"I gasped as the ghost found his way inside of me. I wrapped my arms around his soaking wet body and leaned my head back against the window.

"'This,' said the ghost to his son, 'is how it's done. Watch,' said the ghost, as he began to thrust. 'Watch, and learn.'"

"WHEN IT WAS OVER, when I'd screamed the name my husband and the ghost shared, I made to squeeze my thighs around my lover, to hold him inside of me for a moment longer. But he was gone.

"My legs quivered as I stumbled toward Silas to remove the boot from his chest. I knelt by his side to do the deed and felt the faintest trickle of the ghost's seed dripping out of me. It felt like a betrayal. I prayed that was all that was wasted.

"Then, as if in answer to my prayer, I felt a flutter inside my womb and smiled. 'And there it is,' I told my husband, holding his hand to my belly. 'An end to our suffering and the beginning of our new life. It is done, Silas. I feel our child already.'

"Silas recoiled from me and stalked away. 'Not ours,' he said.

"'Yes,' I protested, standing and reaching for him. 'Ours. No one will know. No one *need* know. The line of Silas Silver will continue.'

"Silas shook his head and shook her off of him. 'Do you want to know something?' he said. 'It was never really about him.'

"I sighed. 'Don't stew over this, Silas. This is a happy day, whatever the circumstances.'

"'I am not stewing,' he told me. 'I am telling you a story. You see, the nightmare, it was never as much about him as it was about *her*.'

"'Your mother?'

"'No!' he shouted. 'Why must my story always be the next chapter of theirs?'

"He reached into his vest pocket and produced an old photo. Then he handed it to me. It was wet now, from where the water-logged boot had soaked the fabric clean through, and Silas seemed broken to see it so.

"'Tamson O'Rourke,' he said as I examined the picture of the pretty young thing. 'Every dream and every nightmare begins with her.'

"'A romance of your youth?' I asked.

"'The romance of my life,' said Silas. 'I dreamt us a beach once, where we spoke the Bard's lines to one another while my foot was borne off on the waves.' He laughed then, though it was mirthless. 'That was the last time I dreamt of my father's godforsaken boot, the last time it haunted me. Soon I was off to war, and dreamt each night of real horrors: visions of musket fire piercing my arms, my chest, delusions of cannon balls taking my legs out from under me.' He closed his eyes, collecting himself, then continued. 'It was Tamson's face that came to me in those moments, not some vision of a boot, not the specter of my long dead father or the memory of my mother and her well-laid plans for me. And it is Tamson's face that has kept me from giving you, or any of the others, what my mother so desperately craved.'

"'My dear, sweet husband,' I said, setting the picture down and taking hold of Silas' hands in my own. 'I had no idea.'

"'You had no reason to know,' he said, looking down, looking away from me.

"'Why do you shun me?' I said, squeezing his hands. 'What I have done, I have done for us.'

"'And what I do,' he said, prizing his hands from mine with a gentleness I was not expecting, 'what I do now, I do for us as well.'

"'And what is that, my love? What will you do for us?'

"'Not us,' he told me, still looking away from me. 'Not you and me,' he said. He nodded at the discarded photograph of his long, lost love. '*Us.*'

"And it was then that Silas looked at me again. But I saw it in his eyes too late to put a stop to it, the look I had seen so often in my father's eyes when he was at last let loose upon a gander.

"My husband wrapped his hands around my throat and squeezed. I fought against him as he strangled me, but it was no use. As he pushed me toward the floor, I reached for the discarded boot, clawing at the floorboards to reach it, but it was just beyond my grasp.

"'Who knows what wicked growth dwells inside of you now?' he spat. 'It may be the spawn of the devil or a mere figment of my tortured imagination, but I will chance neither. If a father I am meant to be, a father I will be. But not this way. Not. This. Way.'

"I slapped at his arms one last time, but he was too much for me. He was too much, and I was too soon gone from this world."

❦

"But not truly gone. Not yet. My spirit still lingered in that room as he let my body slip to the floor, as he plucked the boot from my outstretched hand.

"He held it out before himself and sighed. 'To be, or not to be,' he recited from memory. Then he laughed. A short, pained laugh, but a laugh just the same. 'Oh,' he told the photograph of Tamson, 'it is never a question, my love. At least not one we answer for ourselves.'

"He waited until nightfall to dispose of my body. I spent those hours trying to wrap my ghostly hands around his throat, to do to him what he'd done to me, but I was little more than a shadow. I had no power, and I despaired. Why was I still there? Why was I being made to watch this?

"But then, just as he made ready to rid himself of me once and for all, I got my answer.

"As Silas bent to hoist my body into his arms, he noticed what I noticed. The color had not gone out of me as it should have. And more than that: my belly had swollen since last he'd looked upon me. Swollen considerably, almost as if..."

And here Ada paused to smile wickedly upon Robin. But Robin did not speak. As aghast as she was at this whole tale, as flabbergasted as she was by its ridiculousness, she could tell that Ada believed what she was saying. And if Ada believed it, then maybe just maybe there was a kernel of truth in there somewhere.

"Silas pressed his ear to my still warm flesh and gasped. 'It cannot be.' he said. Then, after a moment, he fell back from my body and clutched at his cheek.

"I looked down upon my body and saw the child moving inside of it. The baby had kicked him. And it was as that particular bit of knowledge dawned on him that my dear husband had himself a spell and slumped unconscious to the floor.

"And that sure was a lucky thing for him, and for all of those blasted Silvers yet to be born, because the shock of what happened next would have struck him dead.

"My body's belly continued to swell, to grow and to grow until it could grow no more. And then I watched, with a mix of delight and horror, as my body opened itself in the way it would have were I still alive. I watched as the child's head emerged. Its shoulders. And then, riding a wave of blood out onto the floor—"

"Please," said Robin, holding up a hand. "Stop."

Ada nodded. "I'm almost done," she said. "There's just a little more you need to know."

❦

"WHEN IT WAS DONE," said Ada, "I felt a hand upon my shoulder. It startled me, for Silas was still on the floor and out like a light, and who else could it be?

"'Ada,' he said, 'it's time to come with me.'

"And for the first time, I laid eyes upon the man who would be my captor."

"The barkeep?" said Robin.

Ada nodded. "But I told him it couldn't be time yet. Did he know what Silas would do when he found this child? This child he would think a demon of some sort, the spawn of the devil himself.

"'Yes,' said the Barkeep. 'I know what he'll do. Which is why we'll take the child with us.'

"'But I'm a ghost,' I told him, as if he didn't know that already. 'How am I—?'

"'Have you tried?' asked the Barkeep.

"'I tried to strangle Silas,' I told him, 'to pay him back for what he did to me.'

"The Barkeep nodded. 'This is different,' said the Barkeep. 'The child is the flesh of your flesh.'

"And so, I knelt to collect the child. And I was stunned to realize that I could hold it in my arms. It was true.

"'I'll get a knife,' said the Barkeep. And when I looked upon him in terror, he smiled kindly. 'For the cord,' he said.

"The Barkeep led me out of the house and along the twilit beach. When I asked him where we were going, he pointed toward a building in the distance that I had never seen in life. It sat beside the Red River: a bar on the bottom floor of a furniture shop."

"This place?" said Robin.

Ada nodded. "He took me in one door, then out another. And when we emerged we weren't on Cape Cod anymore. We were up north. North and west, near where you and I first met.

"The Barkeep led me to a house nearby, told me to lay the child upon the doorstep and to rap the knocker three times. But before I did as I was bid, I asked him if he knew who these people were, if he could make me any promises that the child would be better off here.

"He looked at me and said nothing, let me work out for myself how preposterous the question was. Because how could these people, this family called Gates, do any worse than Silas Silver would have done?"

Robin's mouth fell open.

"Yes," said Ada. "You are the flesh of my flesh."

"And that's why the mirror..." Robin began, then trailed off.

"Yes," said Ada.

"But what about Ryan? The mirror worked on him, too."

"Lot of years since 1892. A Catholic family gets around," she said. "And so did Ryan's grandmother."

"But he and I," said Robin, and she feigned a gag. "We... and he's my... cousin?"

"A distant cousin," said Ada. "Then again, so is your girlfriend. Technically."

"What?" said Robin.

"The baby's father was a Silver, remember.

Robin stood up from the bar. Her head hurt more now than when she'd stumbled in. "This is fucked up," she said. "This is so, so fucked up." Random pieces of the story crashed together inside her head, like that asteroid field in *The Empire Strikes Back*. And she, Robin, was like Han Solo trying navigate her way through it, to find a safe place to land, but the greater part of her brain was like C-3PO and it was shouting at her that the odds of successfully navigating an an asteroid field were approximately 3,720 to 1.

"Sit back down," said Ada. "Don't hurt yourself," she said. "After all, you're my ticket out of here."

"What?" said Robin.

"Yep," said Ada. "My last shot at freedom. Unless you have a kid, of course."

"What about my father?" said Robin. "Or my brother? What about Ryan?"

Ada said nothing, but she looked like she was about to cry.

"Something's going to happen to them?" said Robin. "*All* of them?"

"You're my ticket out of here," said Ada. "*You*."

"No," said Robin, heading for the door. "If you hate the Silvers as much as you seem to, there's no way I'm letting you hitch a ride out of here thanks to me."

"You should hate them too, after all they've done to us. To *you*. After all they're going to do."

Robin's hand was on the door's knob, but she didn't twist it. Not yet. "Going to do?" she said.

"Your brother," she said. "Something's about to happen."

"I'm leaving now," said Robin, holding up a hand. "And don't you dare try and follow me."

"I've already tried," said Ada. "Fifteen years ago."

"At the bar?" said Robin. "That was only thirteen years ago."

"Fifteen years ago now," said Ada. "You've been in here a while."

"I haven't been in here that long," said Robin. "Not two years."

"Time works different in here," said Ada. Then she nodded at the door. "Go ahead and see for yourself. But I'm not lying. It's 2005 outside."

Robin shook her head and said "You're full of shit." Then she opened the door, and a wave of water bowled her over and sucked her out—out onto the now-submerged streets of New Orleans, Louisiana.

14

Ashley was on the third song of her last set when she saw him. She was bent over at the waist, pushing her g-string toward the floor, and there he was: Adam Gates, back for his weekly taste.

At first, all she could see was the shape of him. But that shape was unmistakable, even back there in the most shadowy corner of the club: the slight, feminine expanse of his shoulders; the way that he slouched, like a turtle pulling its head into its shell; the suit that neither fit him nor suited him. Then he stepped into the light, and his face was too much for Ashley to bear. At this distance, he looked like the spitting image of his sister—the sister that Ashley had loved and lost, the woman who'd been gone for two years now.

So Ashley strutted down the catwalk away from him, toward the pole that plunged downward from the ceiling and into the center of the stage. She grabbed hold of it with both hands, at a spot above her head, and pulled herself up. Then she whipped herself around the pole, pulling her knees tight against her chest as she spun—as she spun and spun, closer and closer, to the bottom.

The crowd at the stage hooted and hollered. Back in the shadows, under a cluster of Christmas lights that hung from the ceiling like clusters of grapes from a vine, Adam didn't move a muscle.

AFTER THE SET, back in full costume, she took him by the hand and walked him into the fern-shrouded alcove where she and her co-workers performed their lap dances. She waited for him to sit. Then, much to Adam's surprise, Ashley sat too. She usually preferred to get started right away, to get Adam in and out of there as quickly as she could. But the next girl on stage had picked "Rock You Like a Hurricane" for her first song, and while Ashley's sense of humor could get pretty dark, that song choice was too dark even for her. She couldn't strip to that, not when the city of New Orleans was underwater. In fact, if it wouldn't have gotten her fired, she would've stormed up to the DJ, ripped the disc straight out the player, and hurled it like a shuriken at the new girl's head.

Instead, she swung her legs up and rest them across Adam's lap. Then she asked him if he and the wife had lost power in the storm.

He shook his head.

She nodded. "I suppose," she said, "there wasn't much left of it anyway. By the time it reached us, I mean."

"I suppose," he said.

While they waited for the next song, he ran a hand along Ashley's legs. One leg and then the other, from knee to thigh and back again. But his gaze was elsewhere. His mind, too. Even as he felt her up, Adam was staring up at the tiles of the dropped ceiling—and at the spots where tiles *should* have been. And maybe it was because he was distracted by some detritus up there that he kept not noticing the new stockings Ashley had finally bought (after weeks of him commenting on random runs that no one else ever said shit about). Maybe it was that. Either that, or he no longer cared.

Ashley didn't know which option pissed her off more.

Fortunately, the song was over soon enough and she was up on her feet doing what she did best. And once her gear was gone, stripped from her body and deposited roughly on the floor, she asked him if everything was to his liking.

He smiled and said to her, in his best Dick van Dyke, "Practically perfect in every way."

"Well," she said, affecting an Andrewsian accent, "I shall have to bring my measuring tape with me next time."

"And what might you measure?" he asked.

Ashley didn't answer him, but only because she couldn't up with a comeback—not one from *Mary Poppins*, at least. Instead, she straddled his leg and ground against it.

He asked her if he'd taken it too far.

"It will only have gone too far," she said, "if you attempt to penetrate me with my parasol."

He smiled as she stood and spun slowly on the spot, a music box ballerina built just for him. "Would you like that?" he asked.

"So long as you didn't open it," she said, as she took hold of his knees and lowered her ass onto his lap. "A lady has her limits."

But Ashley didn't have any limits, not really. And she certainly didn't just then, not with that quirky brand of flirting that had always made her wet. She surveyed the club quickly, trying to see if anyone was paying too much attention. And when she felt sure that they weren't being watched, she took the dance further than she ever had before. She pushed her ass against soft linen of his slacks and made circles with her hips. Slow and steady, steady and slow. Slow. And steady.

It wasn't long before she felt his dick throbbing beneath the fabric. And so, to finish him off, she leaned back and rest her head upon his shoulder. She arched her back so that there was room for their heat to pool in the space in between their bodies. Then she turned her face to him and breathed heavy in his ear, nibbled at his earlobe like it was a piece of the fruit she smelled in his hair.

"Holy shit," he said. "Holy—"

Ashley felt him throb against her, felt a violent spurt when he came. And then a second. She almost laughed as his crotch grew sticky and wet. How pent up had he been? Were things *that* bad at home these days? Was his little wifey holding out on him altogether now?

She didn't stop right away, and maybe that was her mistake. He was moaning now—he might've even asked her to stop—but that just drove Ashley more. She squeezed his knees and snapped her hips back and forth. If she was finally going to get something out of this guy—after all these years—then she was going to get *everything*.

Every. Last. Drop.

And then his hands were on her waist, gripping her tightly, trying to hold her in place. But Ashley kept going. She only relented when his hands dropped away. Only when he'd conceded —only then did she still herself. Because maybe this would be the end of it. Maybe she'd finally won, and he would fucking go away for good.

Maybe she'd never have to see him again. And if she never had to see him again, then she'd never have to deal with the ghost of his sister again either—not in the way he stood in the shadows, not in the way he fought to catch his breath when he came, not in the smell of the shampoo Robin and Adam had both been using since their mother left a bottle of it behind when she left them for good.

As Ashley stood to dress, Adam brushed at the legs of his pants—as if trying to sort himself out. Then he mumbled her name, her real name.

Ashley corrected him: "Hannah, sir." In here, in this place, her name was Hannah.

Adam shook his head, pulling the fabric of his pants away from himself. How much had soaked through, and how much was just the wet of his underpants? That's what he seemed to be trying to figure out.

"Shit," he said. "I'm gonna catch hell for this."

"Was the service not to your liking?" Ashley asked him, pouting as she pulled on her panties.

"She's gonna kill me" is what he said. He didn't answer Ashley. Maybe he just couldn't.

She was wrapping her skirt back around her waist when Adam stood and pulled his wallet from his pants. One edge of *it* was wet, too.

"How much do I owe you?" he asked, thumbing through his cash.

"Oh, nothing sir," she said. "That one," she said—and she turned her back to him so she could pat her ass for emphasis—"that one was on me."

༺✿༻

AFTERWARDS—AFTER her shift was done—he was out there, outside, *waiting*.

He'd parked his car in the lot of the Harley dealership around the corner from the club. Had it idling, lights off. Knew that was the way Ashley went home, knew she was living upstairs from her parents now—that she had been ever since Robin disappeared. And he wasn't very subtle about following her, came peeling out of the parking lot once she drove by, almost like he'd dozed off or something and came *this close* to missing her. Ashley was amused. She actually laughed. It had been like this between the two of them, like a game of cat and mouse, since they were kids. For a moment—just a moment, mind you—Ashley remembered why they'd become friends in the first place. The thrill of the chase, of a *game*.

For a moment, she was glad it wasn't over after all.

She didn't take the turn towards home when it came. Ashley drove into Lowell instead, along the boulevard, along the river, until they got to the bandstand across the street from Heritage Farms. Then she pulled over.

The band—his sister and her brother and their pals—they had played on this bandstand once, back in the day. And Ashley remembered crossing the street from Heritage way back then, a frappe for herself in one hand and an orange freeze for her brother in the other. She remembered ranting to Robin about the reverence everyone showed for the supposedly hallowed ground the band walked upon. Was every piece of sod that Gideon's Bible stepped upon somehow sacred?

Robin had laughed then, laughed and mussed Ashley's hair. Then she'd said, "Oh, you Silvers. You're so *dramatic*."

Yes, thought Ashley as she got out of her car, back here in the here and now. *Because all the world's a stage*. How had Robin not known that? *How?* But of course she must've known, because she'd disappeared without a trace—more like a magician than a musician in her final act upon this earth, but a performer never-theless. All the way to the bitter end.

As she crossed the street, Ashley looked both ways for cops—for squad cars or staties patrolling—but there were none. Then, just to be safe, she squinted to see if there was anything to be worried about across the river. When it seemed like the coast was clear, she started toward the stage—to make real the most sacrile-gious idea she'd had in her most sacrilegious life.

Adam followed behind her at a respectable distance. But when Ashley took the stage and started stripping off her sweats—doing her best to look sexy while stepping out of the comfy shit she'd slipped into at the end of her shift—then he picked up the pace. He drew closer and closer, until he stood at the edge of the stage. And that's when he stopped.

She wagged a finger at him.

"I should go home," he said.

Ashley sank to her knees and pressed her hands together like a child in prayer.

"I shouldn't," he said.

She unclasped her hands and pressed them against the stage floor. Then she slid her knees out from under her and sank lower, onto her stomach, and leered up at him, trying to lure him with lasciviousness now, with a more wanton longing. When that didn't work, she pushed her ass up into the air and wagged her tail instead of her finger. And when *that* didn't work, Ashley rolled onto her back and let her head loll over the edge of the stage. She licked her lips as she looked at him from upside down, but still he did not come.

"Oh you," she said to him.

"I've got to go," he said, but he wasn't going anywhere. Ashley knew it. Then he knew it. And then he gave in.

And it was nice at first—a thought that would make Ashley laugh in hindsight, since that sentence could describe both that one night or their entire relationship. It was nice at first, him giving it to her like the animals that all people were deep down inside, deep down beneath the scab no one was brave enough to peel back—that callous called civilization. But then, somewhere in the middle, something changed. Ashley came back to herself, and she asked him to stop.

And maybe he didn't hear her the first time—he was loud as a caveman, for Christ's sake, like he was Fred Flintstone boning Betty Rubble on Swingers Night in old Bedrock—but he for damn sure heard her by the second time.

And, if not the second time, then the sixth. Or the seventh.

15

The road home was a long one for Robin Gates. That she'd made it out of the flooding in New Orleans was a miracle, but her troubles didn't stop there. No. When she finally made it to a rental car lot, money wasn't a problem. But her expired driver's license was. So she had to ask for directions to the nearest bus stop instead. Which she got. But not before answering the question: "Ain't y'all that rock star that went missing a couple years back?"

She nodded and said "Yes, ma'am."

"Where you been?" asked the gal behind the counter, as she wrote down directions.

"To hell and back," said Robin, smiling as she took the slip of paper from the other woman.

"Hell?" said the woman, raising an eyebrow.

"Yep," said Robin, as she made for the door, "There, and back again."

AT THE STATION, while she waited for the next bus to arrive, she stared at a pay phone and tried to think of what she'd say when Ashley picked up—assuming the grimy old thing even worked. Then she realized Ashley had probably moved out of the apartment. It had been two years, after all. And where would she be? At Ryan's place, where she'd crashed during the previous break-ups? At her parents' house, where she went when things weren't working out with Ryan either? Or somewhere else entirely? Maybe she'd gotten a place of her own by now.

Was it too late?

No, thought Robin. *Of course not.* Then a tear welled up in the corner of one of her reddened eyes. *Of course not*, she thought, patting at the wallet in her back pocket and thinking of the slip of paper still hidden safely inside of it. *I still have to die in her arms.*

On the bus north to Boston, dreams of days gone by punctuated Robin's restless fits of sleep. The music video they'd made together, complete with a supermodel guest star for the two of them to fight over. Sharing a pint of Ben & Jerry's in the car on the way to a gig at Great Woods, Ashley spooning a dollop at a time into Robin's mouth while Robin drove. The night in Manila, on the band's tour of Asia—the night Robin met her mother's parents for the first and only time—and the way Ashley rubbed her back in the hotel room that night, until the choking sobs weakened into whimpers, then some more, until the whimpers were gone altogether.

The train ride from Boston back home to Chelmsford on that Tuesday morning four years ago when planes were flying into buildings in other cities and they were evacuated as a precaution. The way they kept their eyes on the Prudential Tower until it disappeared from view, waiting for disaster to strike them the way it had New York and Washington. The flannel she gave Ashley that day because Ash couldn't stop shivering, because her brother was supposed to be on one of those planes—until he and his wife had changed their flight.

Robin had loved that flannel. It had been her dad's, back in the day. But she'd never asked for it back. Not after the first breakup, not after the second, not after the third.

And it was that flannel Ashley was wearing when Robin knocked on the door of the Silvers' house late the next day, when Ashley pulled Robin into her arms and began to cry—to cry harder than Robin had ever seen her cry.

It had already happened, Robin realized. The bad thing that Ada had warned her about. It had already come to pass.

UPSTAIRS IN ASHLEY'S ROOM, they laid in Ashley's bed and held each other—held each other tight as Ashley told the story of what had happened. And though she felt numb throughout most of it, the tale of what happened at the police station brought Robin back to life.

"There was this poster," Ashley began. "There was this poster at the precinct's front door that we stopped to look at after I'd made my statement. We stopped—my mother and me. We stopped, we looked, and I cried. Mum put her arm around me, to kind of nudge me out the door, but I wouldn't move. Robin, we stood there for, like, fifteen minutes. People kept coming in and out, squeezing past us, but I wouldn't move."

When Robin asked her what was on the poster, Ashley told her it was an elephant.

"And when she tried to see what it was about that elephant that made me cry, I told her it was all about the trunk. The ears were cute, as big as Dumbo's—so that, like, if the wind caught them, then he might really fly. And the eyes were gentle—demure —focused on the ground before him and the task at hand. Not on the horizon, not on the future, never on what was to come. But the trunk—that was a beauty too..." Ashley trailed off, searching for the right word. She closed her eyes and found it there.

"Potent," she said. "The elephant's trunk was a beauty too *potent* for me. For my patchwork heart, you know?"

Patchwork. The word reminded Robin of the quilt Ashley had been making out of her old concert t-shirts. Was she still working on it, Robin wanted to know. Even a couple of years later? Or had she stopped? Did the thought of live music remind her too much of Robin's disappearance, of what she'd lost?

"Patchwork," said Ashley, repeating herself. "That's how I think of it, my heart. And I could almost feel the stitching coming loose that night at the precinct, the fabric of the tired thing fraying as love and hope swelled again inside of it.

"An elephant's trunk, I realized, is a hand that'll never be a fist."

Robin asked her to repeat herself, just to be sure of what she'd heard. So Ashley did. And then Robin told her "That's the title of my next album."

"That's not funny," said Ashley. "Not right now."

It was an old joke of theirs. When one of them turned a particularly catchy phrase, the other would say "That's title of my next album." And yes, right now, at this moment, it wasn't the time for jokes. But Robin wasn't joking.

She sat bolt upright and reached for her wallet. Then, finally, after all these years, she let Ashley read the note she'd kept there.

They didn't know whether to laugh or to cry, so they did a bit of both. But then the phone rang, and Ashley crossed the room to answer it.

She took the call with her back to Robin, so it wasn't until Ashley hung up that Robin could see the look on her face. And how pale her face looked.

"What?" said Robin. "Who was it?"

"It was the police," said Ashley, in shock. "My mother, she's... she's been arrested. Or, well, she turned herself in."

"What did she do?" Robin asked.

"She drove across town," said Ashley. "To your dad's house. And she beat the shit out of your brother with a baseball bat."

⚜

SHE DID it in the side yard, with Adam and Robin's father watching from behind the screen door to their porch.

The whole neighborhood watched, in fact—either from their own porches or from positions along the Gates' fence line. The word had gotten out. Everyone knew what Adam had done. And though some thought Ashley had it coming, given her profession, Adam's dad wasn't one of them. Which meant that nobody was going to lift a finger to help the kid, no matter what their personal opinions might have been. That neighborhood listened to Phil Gates. They obeyed. The cops in town—or *enough* of them, at least—they listened to Phil, too. And if he was going to watch his son get what he deserved—if he was going to watch that carnage without raising a finger—then so was everybody else.

When Ashley's mother was done—blood on her hands from the body of a boy whose skinned knees she'd been tending since he took a tumble in the midst of his very first steps—she dropped her weapon to the ground and started back toward her car.

"Doc," said Phil Gates, and the doc, Michaela Silver, turned to face him. Her husband's old classmate, the father of her children's first loves—the only man that anyone in their sleepy suburb had ever really feared—she turned to face him, and she put the fear of God in Phil Gates.

"Yes," she said.

Phil nodded toward the baseball bat. "You best take that with you," he said. "Evidence, you know."

She nodded, then Michaela returned to the scene of her crime. As she crouched to collect her weapon, she tried not to look at what she'd done to the boy. But she couldn't help herself. She shuffled on her knees to Adam and began to palpate his abdomen, his chest. She counted the number of ribs she'd cracked, examined him for the worst of the contusions. Then she looked up at Phil and told him to call an ambulance.

"I will," he said, "as soon as you're gone."

She stood slowly. Reluctantly. And she wondered what she had done.

"Go," said Phil. "Go home, Doc. Wash yourself up, and get back to work. You do good work," he said. "The town needs you."

And so: she went. But she didn't go home. She stopped at the police station and turned herself in. And though no one would corroborate her story, though there would never be any charges filed—though Phil Gates disappeared his son until he was well enough to deny what had happened—Doctor Michaela Silver didn't go back to work for *years*. She *couldn't*.

She'd taken an oath. She'd sworn to do no harm. And even if Phil fucking Gates himself turned up on her doorstep to absolve her, to say, "Well, actually, that's not what the Hippocratic Oath says," she wasn't going to hear it. Ashley's mother knew what she'd promised.

And she knew damn well which promises she'd broken.

❧ IV ❧
THE RIGHT THING TO DO
2005-2006

❦ 16 ❦

W hen they broke up for the fourth time, it was so that Robin could stew in her sadness for a while.

Ashley found her a couple weeks later, in the penthouse of a Vegas hotel, buried beneath a pile of naked dudes and satin sheets. And she was slow to emerge not only because it was hard to untangle the mess of arms and legs and cocks that had fallen asleep on top of her. No, it was not just that. It was also because she couldn't bear to look Ash in the eye, because she hoped she might suffocate under the weight of her man blankets before she had to. Her makeup smeared, her hair a tangled mess, the stench of sweat and semen wafting off her as if propelled by a can of funked up Febreze—it would be just like the good old days, just like nothing had changed at all.

Except that everything had. *Everything.*

Ashley called her name and Robin stirred. The first two boys, the ones wrapped round her legs, fell away as she drew her first deep breath of the morning. Robin watched their heads roll off her stomach, which they'd used as a pillow, and she remembered how they'd fought over her with their tongues. The next to move was the lad who'd fallen asleep across her chest after she'd dotted his i and he'd crossed her t. And last was the fellow she'd used as a pillow herself. As she lifted her head off him and he rolled away, Robin realized he still had his boxers on. In fact, they didn't look stained at all. Robin chuckled, realizing he hadn't been kidding about just wanting to watch. And even as she rubbed at the back of her neck, Robin realized his beer belly was not, in fact, the most uncomfortable pillow on which she'd lain herself down to sleep.

"Hey," said Robin, as she blinked away sleep.

"Hey," said Ashley, a tear in her eye. Then she crossed her arms and pursed her lips. "I see," she said, "that you didn't leave any for me."

ASHLEY TOLD Robin that she didn't want to dance anymore—not for a while, at least—but that she had some other ideas for how to make ends meet. After some cursory googling, they found a camera shop and asked the guy behind the counter what he'd recommend for what they had in mind.

"Just stills?" he asked. "Or you want to shoot video, too?"

Ashley was bent over the glass case where he kept his lenses, and she wasn't paying attention.

"Miss?" he said.

As Ash straightened up, she stuffed her hands into the pockets of a pair of shorts that were too short on her. Too loose, too. The shopkeeper blushed as he noticed—couldn't help but notice, really—that Ashley had nothing on underneath. Robin tried hard not to laugh.

"We'd like to keep our options open." That's what Ashley told him.

BUT, as excited as she was to get started, Ashley was ready to throw the camera at the wall that night. They'd been up for hours searching the web for tutorials, and Ash still couldn't get the hang of it. Robin saw something familiar in the way Ashley gripped the body of that DSLR—which the guy told them was overkill, but which they bought anyway. Ashley clutched that thing the way she used to clutch a video game controller in the seconds before she was going to send it sailing into a wall out of frustration. And so: Robin took it from her, set it on the nightstand, and asked Ashley why she was worrying about it anyway. She was going to be the subject anyway. Robin was going to be behind the camera.

"But what about when you're not here anymore?" That's what Ashley asked, choking on the words. "This year's nearly over," she said. "And next year..."

Robin kneeled between Ashley's legs and took her love's face in her hands. She wanted to say something, wanted to make some promise or other, but there were no promises to make. The end *was* nigh, and even though she'd had years longer than Ashley to get used to that idea, she'd spent precious few of those years coming up with things to say in a moment like this. So she kissed Ashley instead. And she pushed a hand up into the leg of those tiny shorts Ash was wearing, and Ashley fell back onto the bed.

Then Robin pulled those shorts off with one good yank and she kissed Ashley some more.

THE IDEA CAME to them in the morning. They didn't know any pro photographers, but they did know a painter—someone with an eye for composition and lighting and all the rest. He could teach them the basics. And he just happened to live in one of the most beautiful places on earth.

WHILE MICHAEL TAUGHT Robin how to shoot out on the lanai, his wife used their shelf of photo albums to help Ashley scout locations. A few days later, Michael's birthday party did double duty as a kind of graduation ceremony. Ashley got cozy with each of the guests in turn, while Robin stood back and shot pictures of the coziness.

The next day, as Robin was carrying bags out to the rental car, Michael asked if she was working on any new music, or if the new hobby was keeping her too busy.

"I've got a title," she said with a sigh.

Michael smiled. "Some days I wish I was still out there on the road with you," he said.

Robin mussed his hair. "You weren't meant to be a rock star," she said. "And your birthday yesterday is proof of that."

"How so?" said Michael.

"You turned 28," she said. Then she rattled off a list of names, holding up a finger for each. "Kurt," she said. "Hendrix, Joplin, Jones, Morrison."

Michael nodded, remembering. "All dead at 27," he said, his gaze lowered as if out of respect. But then something hit him and he looked Robin dead in the eye.

"What?" she said, but he didn't say anything in reply. Instead, he'd pulled her into his arms and gave her a big old hug. It took her a moment to realize why, but then she hugged him back.

He'd remembered how old *she* was, all of a sudden. And he told her to be careful.

* * *

THE FIRST THING was the beaches. Robin wanted to shoot on every color beach they could find, which included schlepping their gear on a rocky hike to the southern-most tip of the Big Island. In the dark. The *dark!* All so she could be there to capture the sun rising over the green sand of that cove, to watch the light spill across the gooseflesh of a mere mortal and transform her into a golden god.

And it was stunning, that day's shoot. Watching Ashley arching her back on that beach in the early morning light, as if Apollo had driven his chariot all the way down from Olympus to worship *her*—it was beautiful. And it was beautiful not just because Ashley had sculpted her body to meet the ideal of their times. No, it wasn't really because of that at all. It was beautiful because Ashley felt beautiful, no matter what she looked like. It was beautiful because she felt at home in her own skin, at *peace*—maybe more at peace than Robin had ever seen her—and Ashley showed her that. When she moved her body between shots, it was not the striking of one pose and then another. It was not the staccato of Madonna vogueing, trying to invoke Greta Garbo one moment and Marilyn Monroe the next. It was more like her body was a river. Yes. Her body was a river, and Robin was watching the current. That's all she was doing. She was watching a river, a river made flesh, and waiting to capture the beauty of its flow.

In between the beaches, she shot Ashley against backdrops of dark volcanic rock that made it look like they'd flown to the moon and back. She shot her in the torrential rains that lingered over one side of the island and never left. They hiked a mountain until they found winter in paradise, then Ashley took off her top and made the filthiest snow angels Robin had ever seen.

But it was on another island in the chain, at the very end of their trip, that they shot the pictures that they would each remember for the rest of their lives.

ASHLEY'S FINGERS played with the lapels of a half-open robe. The sash dangled to one side, tickling the toes she flexed and unflexed as she waited on Robin.

Behind the camera, Robin adjusted things. In front, Ashley

wondered where Robin had set focus, which small part of her body Robin was going to capture today. This was her job now, and she did it well, but being carved up like a side of beef would always cut her. It would always sting.

A gust of wind whipped off of the lagoon at Kē'ē and through the trees that hid them from the folks gathered on the beach. Ashley shivered as the breeze made goose flesh of her naked skin, but she smiled just the same. It was golden hour after all, and they'd been told there was no better place on Kaua'i to watch the sun set. The regal ridges of the Nā Pali Coast conspired with sea and sky to paint pictures that might make Pele swoon.

If Tūtū were the type to swoon, of course. Which, of course, Ashley remembered—trying to remember how far they were from the nearest volcano—Tūtū was not.

The thought stuck with Ashley as Robin stumbled through her set up: they were carving her up. They were drawing and quartering her. Eighthing her. Sixteenthing.

Ashley closed her eyes and thought of her senior-year English teacher and his lecture about the *blason*, that form of poetry that Shakespeare was making fun of when he wrote that his mistress' eyes were nothing like the sun. The teacher recited Spenser's sixty-fourth in his classroom that afternoon, in his best approximation of the King's English, while Ashley wondered how cute he might be without the aviators and the bushy mustache that were his trademarks. It wasn't until later—until this moment on Kaua'i, maybe—that she'd really thought about the words, that she'd wondered what it must've felt like for an Elizabethan woman in her ridiculous ruff to be picked apart like that. What must it have been like to force a smile when recited to by some overwrought orator, to primp and to preen all in order to be recited about? Not *to*, but *about*.

It was then that Robin broke her reverie. "When you're ready," she said.

Ashley pulled the robe back from her body and let it fall from her shoulders to pool on the ground. Sunlight bathed her now, the last of the day. Robin cursed under her breath. She'd taken too long, and they both knew it. And so, they worked fast. Ashley let her take what she needed, as quickly as she could take it, and she smiled.

And yet, Ashley realized, she smiled not because she'd been told to, not because she *had* to, but because she knew the truth. Someone could tear the pages from magazine after magazine, reassembling them like Shelley's doctor in his lab—or like those kids in *Weird Science*, those two teenage boys wearing bras on their heads in order to conjure Kelly LeBrock—some king could summon all of his horses and all of his men, but they'd never be able to put her together again.

When Robin asked why Ashley was laughing, Ash said that she'd finally decided what she wanted to be for Halloween.

"What?" said Robin, setting a hand upon Ashley's elbow.

Ashley stared at Robin's hand for a moment and stopped laughing. Robin was about to pull it away, but Ashley grabbed it with her free hand and held Robin in place.

"What?" Robin said again, though she'd forgotten what she asking about.

"On Halloween," said Ashley, staring into Robin's eyes with the ferocity she usually reserve for the camera. "On Halloween, I'm going to be Sexy Humpty Dumpty."

Ashley was dead serious for a moment. She give Robin the look that would stop people scrolling on Instagram in the years to come, the look she gave each and every patron at the club when they crowded the catwalk for her sets. She give Robin the look that was meant to say "You, you right there—you've got a shot."

It lasted for but a moment, the look. Then Ashley broke. Then they *both* broke. They laughed so hard that they fell into each other. They fell so hard that they stumbled into the hollow inside of the banyan tree that was their backdrop. Then Ashley fell to her knees and pulled at Robin's clothes until she was just as naked as Ashley had been all along.

They had loved many men between them—and even a few *between* them—but Robin was the only woman Ashley had ever made love with. And it struck Robin in this moment to ask why. So, as Ashley's lips brushed across her leg until hip became thigh, until thigh became loin, Robin asked: "Why me?"

"For when I look at you," Ashley began, in between kisses meant now to prize Robin open, "even for a short time, it is no longer possible to speak."

A moan escaped Robin then that neither of them were expecting. Ashley stopped for a second and looked up with a raised eyebrow, raised to ask if she'd gone too fast. Or too far. Robin covered her mouth and looked about to see if anyone might have seen, might have heard, and she was about to apologize when Ashley finished her quotation.

"It is as if my tongue is broken," said Ashley, and Robin wanted to laugh. Because Ashley's tongue was most certainly *not* broken. But Robin didn't laugh, because she didn't want Ash to stop. Instead, she grabbed a banyan root in each hand to steady herself and she nodded at Ashley to continue. And she did. *God,* she did.

Even if they found every piece of you, Robin thought, *they will never find you. There are bits that even I can't see. That even you can't see.*

But they'll try, Robin thought. *They'll look at these pictures, for years and years—even after your gone—and they'll try. And in that way,* Robin thought, *you will live forever.*

And it was then, even as her body shuddered under the ministrations of the love of her life—it was *then*, with those thoughts, that Robin Gates began writing her final album.

❧ 17 ❧

Sixteen weeks before she was killed, Robin Gates met the man who would kill her.

It was June in Cambridge. Parades of geese and their goslings marched up and down the banks of the River Chuck, eating the grass and shitting on the sidewalk. Runners and cyclists wove through the deposits those foul fowl left behind. A couple of skater boys, too. And across Memorial Drive, a Tai Chi class met in Memorial Park, women in skirts and sneakers power-walking past them and back toward their offices in Harvard Square.

Robin was supposed to be reading. She used to *love* reading. But she'd taken to taking in the world instead, the world she was soon to leave behind.

Beside her, lying facedown on a blanket they'd laid out to keep the geese from laying their own claim, Ashley had fallen asleep in her pursuit of the perfect tan. Robin tried to remember if she'd remembered to apply sunscreen when Ashley asked her to. She reached over Ashley's bare back to grab the bottle of lotion, to examine it for clues, and she'd just begun her investigation when the sun seemed to go out.

Startled, Robin looked up and into the face of a young chap who carried a copy of her latest album under his arm.

"I'm sorry" was the first thing he said. Not "hello," not "excuse me." Nope. Just "I'm sorry." And the way that he said it almost made Robin laugh. His tone of voice reminded her of a sitcom character she and Ashley loved: a hapless paleontologist, forever unlucky in love, whose voice—according to one of his best friends—was capable of inducing suicidal ideation.

"Sorry for what?" said Ashley, who was apparently not as asleep as Robin thought.

"Oh," he said, shifting his weight from one foot to the other. He stuffed his hands into the pockets of his jeans and cast his gaze down at the ground. "I," he stuttered. "I'm... I know it's probably rude to... But I was listening to the album... not this copy of course," he said, nodding towards the sleeved vinyl record under his arm, "but the version on my iPod, and I was thinking, 'Listen to the words, stupid.' I was thinking 'she'd want you to say hello.' I mean..." he began. Then, as he trailed off, he raised his head just enough to look Robin in the eyes. "That's what you were trying to say, right? That was the point of the album, wasn't it?"

Robin, who was kind of sick of the album after months spent making it, wasn't sure it had a point at all. So, instead of answering him, she said "You want me to sign it?"

He nodded, then he handed it over to her.

"You got a pen?"

"Oh," he said, patting at each of his pockets in turn until he found what he was looking for in the front pouch of his sweatshirt. "Yes," he said, handing it over. "I stopped at CVS to get a Sharpie."

"Very prepared," said Robin as she signed the album.

"He must be a Boy Scout," said Ashley, still lying down.

"Huh?" said Robin as she capped the Sharpie.

Ashley rose up onto her elbows then, either unaware of or without a care for the fact that she hadn't yet refastened the top of her bikini. "Be prepared," she said. "It's the Boy Scouts' motto."

But, while Ashley may have paid no heed to the sudden revelation of her décolletage, the Fan certainly did. As quickly as he could, he averted his eyes.

"Wait," Robin said to Ashley, "what's the motto?"

"Nothing," said Ashley, unable to resist the old joke, "what's the *motto* with you?"

The Fan snorted back a laugh. "*The Lion King*," he said, still not looking at them. "That's from *The Lion King*."

"Hey," said Ashley, tugging at the hem of the Fan's sweatshirt. "You can turn around. You're not going to see anything you haven't already seen on the cover."

The Fan turned slowly, his jaw falling as he recognized just who Ashley was. "It's you," he said, pointing at the cover of the album that Robin was handing back to him now.

"Sure is," said Ashley. "Me and an elephant."

Robin held the Sharpie out for the Fan to take, but when he didn't take it right away, she shook it in Ashley's direction. "You want her to sign it, too?"

The Fan backed away, clutching the album to his chest. "No," he said, shaking his head. "I don't want her anywhere near me."

Ashley raised an eyebrow.

"She's dirty," said the Fan. Then he looked at Robin, and he looked like he was about to cry. "You shouldn't be with her," he said. "She's dirty. She'll ruin you."

"Ruin?" said Ashley. "I'll ruin you," she said, then she grabbed the Sharpie from Robin's hand. She hurled it at the Fan—and it would've hit him square in the chest, if not for the album getting in the way. Instead, it hit the album, leaving a dent in the cardboard of the sleeve, then fell to the pavement of the sidewalk, bouncing once and then again until it landed astride a small mound of goose shit.

"You're a whore!" the Fan shouted.

And that's when Ashley stood, still not bothering to put her top back on, and stomped toward him. He was running by the time she'd made it to the now-soiled Sharpie, but not so fast that she couldn't nail him square in the head with it before he was out of range.

Robin half-expected Ashley to shout "Fuck you" after him. Instead, Ash turned around, came back to the blanket, and laid back down to finish her tan.

⚜

SIXTEEN DAYS before she was killed, Robin got a call from her brother's wife. And she should've cried at the news her sister-in-law shared with her, at the phrase "murder-suicide," but the truth was she'd known this was coming. She'd known it ever since her confrontation with Ada at the bar in New Orleans.

Even as Ashley held her afterward, Robin could not bring herself to tears. Not even when Ashley repeated the facts of the story to get them straight in her head.

"Your brother found out he couldn't have kids?"

"Yes."

"Because of the beating my mother gave him for raping me?"

"Yes."

"But he didn't blame my mother," said Ashley. "And he didn't blame me. He blamed your *dad* instead? For letting it happen?"

"Yes."

"And now Adam and your father are both dead," said Ashley.

"Yes," said Robin. She was the last of her family left.

Except for Ryan.

Robin sat bolt upright, Ashley falling away as Robin reached for the phone.

"Who are you calling?" said Ashley.

"Ryan," said Robin. "I need to tell him to be careful."

SIXTEEN HOURS before she was killed, news broke about the death of Ryan Manson. Ashley had just set a pair of plane tickets on the coffee table in front of Robin, telling her this was the way she was going to change the future. "You can't be shot in front of your apartment," said Ashley, "if you're nowhere near your apartment." But as sweet as the gesture was, as much as Robin never wanted to look away from the face of the woman she loved, the flash of BREAKING NEWS across the television screen looming over Ashley's shoulder stole her attention away. And when she saw the portrait of Ryan superimposed over the flaming wreckage of a small plane that had crashed at nearby Logan Airport, it was all she could do to keep from passing out. She pointed over her shoulder and waited for Ashley to react.

"Are you fucking kidding me?" she screamed, at both the news that the airport would be closed until notice and at the ludicrousness of "destiny" pushing back at them once again. But it was naught but a moment before anger and shock gave way to sadness, naught but a moment before Ashley sunk to her knees and fell back into Robin's waiting arms to weep. They had both loved Ryan, but Ryan had been Ashley's for longer than he'd been Robin's. During each of Robin and Ashley's breakups, it had been into Ryan's arms that Ashley had retreated.

"I know," said Robin, but what she knew even she didn't know. Did she know anything anymore? Anything except the inevitability of the fate they'd arrive at the next day?

"Maybe there's a flight out of Manchester," Ashley stuttered between sobs. "Or Providence." But she offered these solutions without any real hope in her voice, as if she had finally accepted the truth of it—that there was nothing they could do.

SIXTEEN MINUTES before she was killed, it was still September 28. So Robin and Ashley decided they'd take one last stroll along the river.

"Or," said Ashley, pointing through the window as she waited for Robin to tie her shoes, "we could go get drunk at the new bar across the street."

"What new bar?" said Robin, striding across the bedroom in her still unlaced sneakers.

But she knew which bar it would be even before she made it to the window. It was a dive, just as it always was—just as it always would be—just a dive bar built into the basement of a building where there'd been no bar the day before.

"And," said Ashley, "check out the uniform on the chick out front. Who is she supposed to—?" said Ashley, but she trailed off as she realized *exactly* who the chick out front was supposed to be. Who she *was* for sure.

"Ada," said Ashley, and she hated the sound of the name as she said it. Hated the taste of those two syllables on her tongue.

Robin sat on the bed with a sigh of resignation and got back to tying her shoes. Then she told Ashley she had to let it happen. This was it. This was the only way to save the Silvers. Remember what Ada said, Robin reminded her. "I'm her ticket back to life," she said. "And she wants revenge on the whole lot of you."

"What if I just run across the street and kill her instead?" said Ashley, and she growled as she said it. "I could strangle her with my bare hands."

"She's already dead," Robin reminded her.

Ashley stared out the window again. "I don't see a gun on her."

Robin stood and put a hand on Ashley's shoulder, then another hand on the other shoulder. And she waited, she waited until Ashley was ready to face her—until Ashley was ready to face the facts.

"Can't we just stay in here?" said Ashley. "Can't we just go back to bed and stay there for the rest of our lives?"

Robin shook her head. "The rest of my life is right outside that window," she said. "And we both know there's no denying that. We've tried, and it doesn't work."

"What about the rest of my life?" said Ashley.

"Well," said Robin. "All I know is that it starts in the same place that mine ends. And I can't wait to see what you do with it."

"But you'll be dead," said Ashley.

Robin nodded toward the window. "Remember Ada," she said. "Dead isn't what it used to be."

৩২৩

SIXTEEN SECONDS before she was killed, on the stoop of their apartment building, Robin felt a tug at her sleeve. Ashley was pointing to the right, pointing at a man rounding the corner of their block and stepping out of the shadows.

"It's him," said Ashley, and Robin didn't have to look twice to see that it wasn't just "him," the guy who was going to kill her, but *him*—a guy they'd met before.

The Fan still had the album under his arm. Robin wondered if he'd kept it there for the past four months. She wondered if he'd changed in that time, since it looked like he was wearing the same sweatshirt. The same jeans. Maybe he didn't even have anything to change into. That occurred to Robin now, too.

But she didn't have any more time for things to occur to her, because Ashley was stepping forward now and trying to get in the way. And the Fan was dropping the album to the ground in front of him. Then he was stepping on it, the vinyl cracking under his weight—and the weight of his anger—as he raised his gun. But the Fan wasn't pointing the pistol at Robin. The Fan was pointing it at Ashley.

Across the street, at the top of her lungs, Ada screamed "DO IT!"

But before he could do it, before he could squeeze that trigger and quench Ada's thirst for revenge, Robin stopped him with a fist to the side of his face.

The Fan fell to the ground, clutching at his jaw. And there were tears in his eyes as he tasted the blood spilling from his now split lip, as he caught sight of his blood on Robin's closed fist. Tears brought on by physical pain, yes. But tears sprung of a deeper hurt as well. The Fan's eyes darted from the sight of Robin's bloodied flesh to the sight of his ruined record, to the text scrawled across the sleeve—the promise he saw in those words. *A Hand That Will Never Be a Fist?* That was all bullshit, he realized now. All of it. Like everything else.

And so it was that he finally pointed his weapon at the woman he was meant to kill all along. And so it was that he shot Robin once, and then again. And then again.

He screamed the word "HYPOCRITE!" at her as she fell back against the brick wall of her apartment building. Then he dropped the gun and he ran.

Across the street, just before she and her bar vanished into the night, Ada shouted "NO!"

And on a sidewalk in Cambridge, Massachusetts, a few minutes past midnight on September 29, 2006, Robin Gates died in the arms of the woman she loved.

18

I t's a strange thing to watch someone you love go on to love someone else, but that's just what Robin did while she waited for an answer to her knock on heaven's door. And of course Ashley was so full of love to give that it wasn't just one person she fell for. It was nearly every person she met—every person who wasn't an outright shithead that is. It was like she saved up all the love Robin had given her over the years and now that burden was too heavy to bear. So she was giving it all away, every last drop of it, to just about anyone who expressed an interest.

But what made Robin sad, as she sat in a darkened corner of Ada's bar and snuck peeks behind the black-out curtains when Ada wasn't looking—what made her sad was the way Ashley refused any love she was offered in return.

Ada slapped at Robin's hand and drew the curtains shut again. "It'll come to her when she's ready," said Ada.

"How do you know? How do you know she won't give every piece of herself away until there's nothing left?" said Robin.

Ada frowned. "Because she's a Silver," she said. "They're survivors."

"Not like us," said Robin, sipping at her beer.

"Not like me," said Ada. "But you," she said, "you're more than just the flesh of my flesh, remember." And now she smiled. "You're the flesh of their flesh, too."

And Robin could swear there was a flicker of hope in Ada's eyes as she turned to get back to her business.

"What are you up to?" Robin shouted after her ancestor, after the vile woman who had become the villain of her story.

"Nothing yet," Ada called back over her shoulder. "But give me time," she said. "Give me time."

ॐ

The Silver Family's story continues in The Elixir of Denial, *wherein Ashley tries to forget about Robin by fucking her way across the space-time continuum—and ends up discovering she might have more than one true love, after all.*

ACKNOWLEDGEMENTS

Chapter 5 is essentially an alternate take on the short story "After the Prom," which first appeared in my collection *All He Left Behind*. Some of the material will be familiar to those who read that book, but much of it will be brand new.

Portions of Chapter 13 were first performed as the stage play "The Boot" at the Players' Ring in Portsmouth, New Hampshire as part of their first ever *Evening of Grand Guignol*, which ran from July 6–15, 2012. Silas was played by Chuck Galle and Ada was played by Erika Wilson. "The Boot" first appeared in prose form on Clarkwoods.com, then later as part of my novella *The Seven Wives of Silver*.

The final section of Chapter 16 was first published, in slightly different form, as "Together Again" in the 2019 issue of *Commonthought*.

This book features more scenes inspired by my real life than the previous two Stains of Time books combined. Because of that, it seems like an opportune time to repeat the disclaimer from the Copyright page of this book: "Names, characters, places, and incidents either are the product of the author's imagination or are used fictitiously."

If you know me, or have known me in days gone by, and you see a bit of yourself in these pages, please know that I draw from my memories with love and affection, and that every character here is a composite of many people I've known.

Except for the people I totally made up, of course.

My point: I didn't write any of these characters as a way of "getting back" at someone. I wrote, as always, to understand and to connect—to make peace with feelings I didn't examine fully enough the first time around.

Special thanks to Lissa Brennan, Ali Russo, and Bethany Snyder for their invaluable feedback on early versions of this manuscript.

Thanks to my brother John Clark for his help with the copy-editing. Any remaining errors are the result of my own stubbornness or stupidity.

And thanks to my wife Stephanie, who listened to me read aloud the final drafts of these chapters as I was finishing them.

ABOUT THE AUTHOR

E. Christopher Clark is the author of the Stains of Time series, a family saga with a hint of magical realism and a whole lot of time travel. His other books include the short story collections *Out of the Woods* and *Under the World*, the novella *The Seven Wives of Silver*, and a collection of poems cheekily titled *Bad Poetry Night*. His short stories have been published in *Live Free or Ride: Tales of the Concord Coach*, *River Muse: Tales of Lowell & the Merrimack Valley*, and the University of Hawaii's *Vice-Versa*. A graduate of Lesley University's MFA in Creative Writing program, he lives in Massachusetts with his wife and daughters.

echristopherclark.com

facebook.com/eccbooks
x.com/eccbooks
instagram.com/eccbooks
goodreads.com/eccbooks
pinterest.com/eccbooks
amazon.com/E.-Christopher-Clark/e/B00H0G94T0